WIN, LOSE OR DRAW

PETER CORRIS is known as the 'godfather' of Australian crime fiction through his Cliff Hardy detective stories. He has written in many other areas, including a co-authored autobiography of the late Professor Fred Hollows, a history of boxing in Australia, spy novels, historical novels and a collection of short stories about golf (see www.petercorris. net). In 1999, Peter Corris was awarded the Lifetime Achievement Award from the Crime Writers Association of Australia and, in 2009, the Ned Kelly Award for Best Fiction for *Deep Water*. He is married to writer Jean Bedford and has lived in Sydney for most of his life. They have three daughters and seven grandchildren.

Peter Corris's Cliff Hardy novels include *The Empty Beach*, *Master's Mates*, *The Coast Road*, *Saving Billie*, *The Undertow*, *Appeal Denied*, *The Big Score*, *Open File*, *Deep Water*, *Torn Apart*, *Follow the Money*, *Comeback*, *The Dunbar Case*, *Silent Kill*, *Gun Control* and *That Empty Feeling*. *Win, Lose or Draw* is his forty-second and final Cliff Hardy book.

He writes a regular weekly column for the online journal *Newtown Review of Books* (www.newtownreviewofbooks. com.au).

PETER CORRIS

WIN, LOSE OR DRAW

ALLEN&UNWIN
SYDNEY · MELBOURNE · AUCKLAND · LONDON

Thanks to Jean Bedford, Sofya Gollan, Vincent Hawkins,
Gaby Naher and, for yachting information, Mark Killeen and
Dr Philip Nitschke.

Also a special thanks to Patrick Gallagher, Angela Handley,
Jo Jarrah, Ali Lavau, the publicists and the sales and marketing
team at Allen & Unwin for being so helpful and supportive
over many years.

This is a work of fiction. Names, characters, places and incidents are products of the author's imagination or are used fictitiously. Any resemblance to actual events, locales, or persons, living or dead, is entirely coincidental.

First published in 2017

Copyright © Peter Corris 2017

All rights reserved. No part of this book may be reproduced or transmitted in any form or by any means, electronic or mechanical, including photocopying, recording or by any information storage and retrieval system, without prior permission in writing from the publisher. The Australian *Copyright Act 1968* (the Act) allows a maximum of one chapter or 10 per cent of this book, whichever is the greater, to be photocopied by any educational institution for its educational purposes provided that the educational institution (or body that administers it) has given a remuneration notice to the Copyright Agency (Australia) under the Act.

Allen & Unwin
83 Alexander Street
Crows Nest NSW 2065
Australia
Phone: (61 2) 8425 0100
Email: info@allenandunwin.com
Web: www.allenandunwin.com

Cataloguing-in-Publication details are available
from the National Library of Australia
www.trove.nla.gov.au

ISBN 978 1 76029 478 6

Internal text design by Emily O'Neill
Set in 12/17 pt Adobe Caslon by Midland Typesetters, Australia
Printed and bound in Australia by Griffin Press

10 9 8 7 6 5 4 3 2 1

The paper in this book is FSC certified.
FSC promotes environmentally responsible,
socially beneficial and economically viable
management of the world's forests.

For Jean
The first one was for her and so is the last

And the losers now will be later to win.

—Bob Dylan, 'The Times They Are a'Changin"

part one

part two

1

I'd read about it in the papers, heard the radio reports and seen the TV coverage and then forgotten about it the way you do with news stories. For a couple of weeks or so the image of fourteen-year-old Juliana Fonteyn was never out of the heads of anyone who paid attention to the media.

Juliana attended an exclusive private school, Chelsea College, in the eastern suburbs. With her father, businessman Gerard Fonteyn, and stepmother Sonja, nee Bartholomew, and her brother Foster, eighteen, she lived in Vaucluse in a waterfront property that had its own beach, wharf, pool and spa, and five-car garage. At fourteen, Juliana stood 178 centimetres tall, had the face of a fashion model, was a high-performing athlete, and a talented musician with an IQ of 150. She was, by all accounts, a friendly, unassuming, rather serious-minded girl.

One day in December, during the school holidays, she disappeared while her father was at his office, her stepmother was attending a charity event and her brother was doing whatever eighteen-year-old boys on holiday do. None of the servants—maid, cook or gardener—was live-in. Her father, first to come home, found her gone. Her mobile phone and iPad were still in the house; her bicycle was in the garage. Her three swimming costumes were in her room and the clothes she'd been wearing when her father last saw her—shorts, a T-shirt and sandals—were missing. She'd announced her intention to 'veg out' for the day.

Juliana had scarcely had a day's illness in her young life. She'd received ten dollars a week pocket money when she reached ten years of age and she'd had two five-dollar increments since. She paid for her own iPad downloads and the DVDs she bought or hired. She had perfect vision and perfect teeth.

Naturally, I didn't absorb all this from the media. I hadn't paid that much attention at the time and more than a year went by after the disappearance before the matter came my way. I got this information and a lot more from Gerard Fonteyn OA when he hired me to find his daughter.

'I won't pretend you're the first investigator I've approached, Mr Hardy,' Gerard Fonteyn said when we met at his office in Double Bay. He'd phoned the day before and we'd agreed on the time and place. My business was in a slump and I'd had to give up my rented office in Pyrmont. I was working from home and had moved a desk and filing cabinets into the upstairs front room. I'd cleaned the carpet and the windows and had the room painted. But it reeked of STO—small time operation—and I was glad of Fonteyn's suggestion of where to meet.

'I don't imagine so,' I said. 'I'm not on the A-list and probably barely make the B-list.'

We were sitting around a coffee table in a sort of alcove to his spacious office—wood panelling, air-con, discreet lighting. A slim young woman, impeccably dressed, had served us coffee. Fonteyn waved my response away.

'One on the A-list, as you call it, tried hard with no result; another charged me for doing nothing. A third, I suspect, intended to exploit me in some way. They had nice suits and offices. You have a reputation which is worth more than ... the trappings.'

When he said that I couldn't help looking around the room. I drank some of the excellent coffee and didn't say anything. Neither did he.

Gerard Fonteyn was forty-nine and the CEO of a company that bore his name. My quick research following his initial phone call told me that he owned various interlocking enterprises: beauty parlours that related to fashion boutiques and high-end catering services; holiday resorts that tied in with an interest in cruise ships, recreational boat and plane operations and ecotourism.

'I'm a very wealthy man,' he said after this silence, 'but since my daughter disappeared I've felt like a pauper. Can you understand that?'

'Not sure.'

'I understand you have a daughter.'

'I do,' I said. 'But I didn't know about her until she was almost an adult. We're very close now and I have grandchildren, but it all feels more like . . . a friendship than the kind of attachment you're talking about.'

Juliana had got her looks from her mother, who had died of cancer when she was five. Fonteyn was barely of medium height and heavily built with a high colour. At a guess he kept the flab under control with exercise, diet and steam baths and would always have to. He had a good head of hair above a fleshy face that sagged in spots.

'You may be lucky in that,' he said. 'But my situation is very different. I couldn't believe that a creature as wonderful as Juliana could be created by me and I cannot accept her loss.'

I nodded. He must have spent thousands on having flyers printed and distributed and on full-page newspaper ads and television spots. He'd announced a $250,000 reward for any information leading to the whereabouts of his daughter.

'Other than that . . . inability to accept,' I said, 'is there any solid evidence that she's still alive?'

He hadn't touched his coffee. Now he picked up his cup and drained it in two gulps. 'I'm encouraged,' he said.

'How's that?'

'Every other investigator I've spoken to has been so eager to get the commission that they haven't asked that sort of basic question. The answer is no. I established a website people could contact with information but all I've had are crank theories, false sightings and foul accusations.'

'Accusations?'

'Of course. As you must know, the first suspect in a case like this is the father. I don't know how often that turns out to be true, but you wouldn't believe some of the unspeakable suggestions sick minds out there have made.'

'Juliana showed no signs of disturbance . . . dislocation?'

He hesitated. 'A couple of years ago I would have said none. She was a happy, well-adjusted child who got on well with me, her brother, Foster, and her stepmother. There were the usual mood swings at puberty, tiffs with friends, food fads and the like but nothing . . . troubling. But then she seemed to become moody and bad-tempered all the time. Nothing we did was right. We didn't worry too much about it, just waited for her to grow out of it . . .'

'I'll be honest with you, Mr Fonteyn. The likelihood is that your daughter was abducted opportunistically and has been killed and disposed of.'

'No!'

'But just perhaps not. Just perhaps something else happened. The trail, if there is one, is very cold and well-trodden but I'm willing to make a preliminary . . . provisional investigation.'

'Provisional?'

'If I think I can't make any progress I'll tell you so the minute I decide, and I'll only charge you *pro rata.*'

'You can't imagine that I'm concerned about your charges.'

'No, but I am. I don't exploit people and you've laid yourself wide open for exploitation from your . . . emotional attitude. It's no wonder you've come under suspicion. You'll remain that way while this case is open.'

'D'you mean you'll regard me as a suspect?'

'Of course.'

'Jesus, you're direct.'

'There's no other way. Have you changed your mind?'

Despite the air-conditioning he was sweating in his collar and tie with his suit coat buttoned. He reached for a napkin that had come with the coffee and blotted his forehead.

'Not at all,' he said. 'You're a difficult man to deal with, but I suppose that's a good thing in your profession.'

'I think so,' I said. 'I have to tread on toes, starting with yours.'

For the first time he smiled. 'I think I can see how that plays out. Keeps you off the A-list though.'

'Right,' I said.

2

I told Fonteyn I'd send him a contract that'd stipulate my usual retainer and daily rate plus expenses and the terms I'd outlined. Before I left he went to a filing cabinet and pulled out the largest set of material—notes, photographs, newspaper clippings and DVDs of television treatments of Juliana's disappearance—I've ever received from a client. It was all in a box file, centimetres thick, with a padded section for the discs and photographs. A quick glance showed me that the list of addresses and telephone numbers that began the file covered two closely typed sheets.

My first stop on the way home was the Fonteyn house in Vaucluse. It was a warm day in February and I stood on a high point north of the house and used binoculars to get the details. Two storeys of white brick on a large block, most of an acre in the old money, with trees, shrubs and flowerbeds all artistically placed. From my vantage point I could only get a glimpse of the edge of the balcony that afforded the residents a view of the water. It looked to be wide enough to have a game of table tennis without risk of losing the ball.

A metal staircase zig-zagged down the cliff to the jetty and the beach. A motor launch, modest in size compared to some you see and with a dinghy attached, was moored at the jetty. Bordered by rocks at either end, the small, white-sand beach was inaccessible except via the house or by water. That water, this being Sydney Harbour on a perfect day, was similarly perfect.

The house had the usual high brick wall with a wide security entrance—a booth with a heavy gate was set into the wall. It had a tiled roof and no doubt everything needed in the way of intercom connection and CCTV. Getting in there wouldn't be easy unless you were wanted.

I drove to Chelsea College in Bellevue Hill. The property sprawled along a stretch of high ground a couple of blocks back from the bluffs. Again, top security all around and high maintenance: tennis and basketball courts, a hockey or soccer field, and if that long, low building sparkling in the sunshine didn't house a swimming pool, a gym and a squash court I'd be very surprised. The school itself seemed to comprise several buildings connected by covered breezeways. Architect-designed structures, no demountables of the kind I'd spent the greater part of my schooldays in.

My meeting with Fonteyn had been at 11.30 so after that and my check on the house it was past 1.30 and school was back in. I made my surveillance quickly. These days, checking out a school through field glasses is a sure way to attract attention and trouble.

Fairly or not, in the current climate of anxiety about child abuse, teachers come under scrutiny. I thought it likely that some would be mentioned in earlier investigators' reports, and I wanted a look at their work situation.

There was a large car park shaded by trees and difficult to see in detail. After some fiddling with the focus I realised that it was divided into two sections—one for staff and one for students. I laughed out loud when I saw this. About a dozen or so boys in my final year, including me, drove cars to school. No girls did. We parked them well away from the school because we were all unlicensed, we were all under age, and at least half of the cars were unregistered. The rest were 'borrowed' without parental permission. I drove a battered Falcon a mate and I had 'restored'. We shared it until it suffered a fatal collapse. I've been a Falcon man virtually ever since.

The teachers' section held mostly family sedans, SUVs and station wagons. The students' area, containing about twenty vehicles, featured new looking VWs, hatchbacks and sporty models of one kind or another. I couldn't help wondering what kind of car Fonteyn would have bought Juliana when she got her P plates—maybe a modest little Alfa.

Driving home I admitted to myself that I'm prejudiced against the rich. They are too few to have so much when so many have so little. I didn't really want to take the Fonteyn matter on, even though I'd liked him well enough and his treatment of me had been fine. But I needed the work and the money. Then there was the elephant in the room. Fonteyn had made it clear that the reward was still on offer. Two hundred and fifty grand would make me solvent and able to pick and choose my jobs. The rich have their uses.

It was a Tuesday. A lot of my cases have begun on Tuesdays. The client thinks it over hard on the weekend, makes the call on Monday and sets up a Tuesday meeting. Rich or not so rich, the pattern is the same. I'd been to the gym on Monday as usual and felt virtuous. I'd taken my grandsons Jack and Ben for an early dinner in Newtown at the Italian Bowl: spaghetti bolognaise for them with heaps of parmesan cheese, pesto gnocchi for me and gelato after—for them. One glass of white with the food and a short black while they wolfed down the gelato. Then I took them back home to receive the gratitude of my daughter Megan and her partner Hank for having given them an hour and a half off. More virtuous feelings and so to bed, as whatsisname said.

Next day, I spent the morning cleaning the decks for a clear field to look at the Fonteyn case. I spread the contents of the box file out over the desk, covering most of the surface, pushing the Mac screen and keyboard aside to make space.

There were several photographs of Juliana, including the one that had appeared in the press, on letterbox flyers and on TV. It was a full-length shot of her in mid-stride wearing jeans and a long-sleeved T-shirt, carrying what looked like a gym bag and with her mane of honey-blonde hair slightly disturbed by her movement and the wind.

It was a spontaneous, unstudied picture that somehow captured the essence of her beauty—her youth and yet the beginnings of something else, her innocence but also a potential for experience. She was a young Charlotte Rampling, a junior Maria Sharapova.

Reports by other investigators bulked large along with hundreds of newspaper clippings, printouts of blogs and transcripts of radio reports. There were printouts of messages on Fonteyn's web page, some of which had been followed up to no result. There were printouts of several rancid tweets speculating about Juliana's lubricity and Fonteyn's sexual predilections.

Particularly offensive was something I imagine must have given Gerard Fonteyn nightmares. A photo of a life-sized cardboard model of Juliana, based on the familiar photograph, had been erected at various points around the eastern suburbs. One of these had been graffitied and mutilated in a way that could only be described as demented. Accompanying the picture of this atrocity were police statements about their investigations of what they termed an 'incident', meaning deposits of sperm on the cutout, which had been analysed without anything being learned. Following this, the models had been quickly withdrawn.

I worked through the newspaper coverage and saw the story slowly diminish in importance as other triumphs and tragedies appeared—flaring up as a reporter took an interest, dying away, being revived again to mark six months and a year after the disappearance, and finally stopping altogether.

David Cork, a reporter for the online news survey *The Dark Side*, appeared to have stayed with the story the longest. I checked with the list and his name and mobile number were there. I flicked through the previous investigators' reports and saw that, with one exception, they were useful only in identifying people worth talking to, backgrounding Fonteyn, his son and second wife and the servants but not coming up with anything that cast any light on what happened in broad daylight on that December day. The exception was an investigator's interview with Juliana's brother, Foster. His attitude was described as 'uncooperative and abusive'.

The names of teachers, friends, a tennis coach and a maths and physics tutor were listed. Juliana got high marks in all subjects except maths and physics, for which she expressed an extreme distaste. I'm with her. I assumed all these people had been interviewed by the police and that contact was my obvious starting point.

Detective Superintendent Rupert Seymour, head of the Missing Persons Division of the police service, was in charge of the case—a measure of the weight Fonteyn could swing. I didn't know him but I had a card to play—Frank Parker, a former Deputy Commissioner, stood high in the esteem of the service and was an old friend of mine. Our friendship, bruised and battered by my indiscretions, was still intact, if slightly more distant than it had once been. I was confident Frank could get me access to Seymour.

It took the best part of two days and several phone calls to set that meeting up. I spent the time working through the file and watching the television reports. I also did some research of my own on Fonteyn. He was English of French Huguenot extraction and had met an Australian student when they were both doing degrees in chemistry at Cambridge. He married her, came to Australia and devised a skin cream that took the cosmetics world by storm.

Fonteyn had translated that success into an interlocking empire, as I knew from the press coverage at the time of his daughter's disappearance. My probing revealed that he had topped up his first-class bachelor's degree with a PhD earned inside two years while simultaneously earning an MBA. He'd rowed for Cambridge and had successfully participated in a mass swim of the English Channel. His then wife, also holding a first-class degree, had been the model for early promotions of his skin cream. Even on the dusty screen of my Mac her image glowed.

*

I turned up to the Darlinghurst police headquarters on time, respectably dressed and prepared to be deferential to the big brass. There was no need, as I had just a few minutes with Seymour. He explained that he'd only been nominally in charge of the investigation to placate Fonteyn and that Detective Inspector Tom Cartwright had done the heavy lifting.

Seymour introduced me to Cartwright and we went from a large, well-appointed office to a smaller, plainer one. Cartwright was in his late forties, tall and spare with a dry, humourless manner. After a short, mock fossick, he produced a file, not as thick as the one I had from Fonteyn, from a drawer, put it on the table in front of him and brought his fist down on it quite hard. Obviously I was not going to see inside it. He'd been briefed on what I wanted.

'You're wasting your time, Hardy,' he said.

'Oh? Why d'you say that, Inspector?'

'The father did it.'

3

'It's obvious,' Cartwright said. 'The man was obsessed with her, worshipped her. He thought she was the reincarnation of his first wife.'

'How did you learn this?'

He deliberated whether to answer but eventually did. 'From the son.'

'Is he a reliable source?'

'And the stepmother.'

'Same question.'

'We got a psychologist in.'

I'd seen a couple of doctors' names on Fonteyn's list. I wondered whether one of them was the psychologist and that made me wonder how much of the police investigation had been made available to Fonteyn or the earlier investigators. I asked Cartwright whether he'd cooperated with them.

'Minimally,' he said. 'You seem to be a special case, having Frank Parker's support, but I can still use my discretion about what I tell you.'

'Fair enough. Just a few questions then. Wasn't Fonteyn at work all day?'

Again he paused to consider. 'He can come and go from his office whenever he likes without anyone necessarily seeing him. His secretary was off sick. He could answer the phone or not as he pleased. There was no one to keep tabs on him for most of the day. Besides . . .'

'Besides what?'

Cartwright seemed keen to convince me that I should go away and not bother him. 'It's not entirely clear when the kid was last seen. The servants didn't clock in until mid-morning. The wife had been out late the night before and slept in. So, apart from the father, who said he'd seen her at breakfast, there was no verifiable sighting of her from the evening before when, again according to the father, she went to bed early.'

'This expression "veg out" she's said to have used. Who supplied that?'

'The father again, allegedly quoting her.'

'What about the son?'

'What about him?'

'When did he last see his sister?'

He consulted the file. 'The night before, like the father. The son took off at sparrow-fart the next day. Has his own car.'

'She didn't phone or text or whatever else they do?'

'No.'

'Was that unusual?'

He shrugged. 'Apparently not. She wasn't a great one for the . . . social media. She read a lot, especially in the holidays, and was serious about her sports She valued her sleep. I wish I could say the same of my kids.'

'What d'you think happened?'

'I don't like to think.'

From the way he spoke I could tell that he'd taken the matter seriously; he'd worked at it and it had worked on him.

'You've wrapped it up in your own mind, Inspector. You must have a theory.'

He sighed and leaned back in his chair, bringing his hands to his head to stroke his thinning hair as if he knew the case had eroded and reduced him. 'Fonteyn has a boat. He's a strong, fit guy and there's a very, very big stretch of water right on his doorstep.'

I absorbed this. 'What were your impressions of Fonteyn?'

'I only met him once, briefly.'

I stared at him. 'But you were the investigator. You must have reported to him on progress, or lack of it, got the list of names and so on.'

'I got the names but I didn't report to him. I reported to the Super, who reported to Fonteyn.'

He spoke with some heat. Clearly he'd resented the kid-glove treatment Fonteyn had received.

'Did he do a lie-detector test?'

'He passed it. The guy's a near genius, I'm told. People like that can beat the polygraph.'

I nodded. 'But you met the stepmother?'

'Again, briefly. That was pretty hands-off as well.'

'But your impression?'

His thin mouth turned down at the corners. 'Icy, top-drawer type. No time for the girl or her brother. Riding the gravy train.'

'So you think Juliana's dead?'

'I do. I'm sorry, sounds like she was a good kid for someone born with the silver spoon, but that's what I think.'

'And you don't believe we'll ever know for sure who did it?'

'Not unless she pops up, trussed with Fonteyn's old school tie.'

'The heat's off. If he did it why would he hire me at this late stage?'

He went to the file again and flicked through several documents until he found the one he wanted. He did it impatiently, weary of being questioned. I'd got everything I'd get from him. 'Talk to the psychologist, this Dr Anna Rosen. She'll fill you in.'

He read off a mobile number and slammed the file shut. I thanked him and left. We didn't shake hands.

*

I was intrigued but not convinced by Cartwright's certainty. It could've been based on frustration at not making progress with the case, or resentment at the subsidiary role he'd been forced to play. It certainly wasn't based on an assessment of Fonteyn. From the sound of things, he'd not spent much more time with him than I had. I needed more information to get my bearings in the case and there were choices to be made about where to find it.

When in doubt, have a drink. I'd caught a bus that had dropped me a longish walk from the Darlinghurst HQ because I needed the exercise and parking around there is impossible. I wandered back to Crown Street and found a wine bar that provided sandwiches and light meals. I ordered a BLT and a glass of red and sat looking out at the passing parade—the suits, male and female; the youngsters, pale and dark, some tattooed and pierced, others more conformist; the old, discernibly slower than the young but many looking happier.

'Hello, Cliff. What are you doing in these parts? Reminiscing?'

Ruby Thompson lowered her ample backside onto a chair at my table. Ruby was the madam of a Kings Cross brothel whom I'd had hands-off dealings with back when I had my office in St Peters Lane. Ruby was a fund of knowledge about the working girls and in those days, when I was dealing with the 'faces' of the area, she was very useful. I never allowed her information to get back to the street and once or twice I did her favours and we became friends.

'No, Ruby. I've just come from visiting the cop shop. Can I buy you a drink?'

'Got a drop coming, thanks anyway. How's things?'

'Tight, as the actress . . .'

'Don't. It's not funny at my age. I heard you've got a couple of grandkids.'

'Now how would you know that?'

'Never mind. Boys or girls? How old?'

'Boys, ah, eight, I think, and about three and a bit, roughly.'

'Typical. I've got a couple as well. One of them wants to be a doctor, would you believe. Jesus, what I've seen of doctors . . .'

'What you've paid them.'

'Yes, well anyway, this one's got his heart set on being a doctor but he's weak at maths. That's what brings me here . . . oh, thanks, love.'

A small carafe of white wine and a modest sandwich had arrived. Ruby, a bit over-dressed as always, shook off the silk scarf she'd been wearing over a silk dress with ruffles and shimmering gold flecks, and watched me as I poured her wine.

'Ever the fucking gentleman,' she said, 'but never the . . .'

'Let it go, Rube. We had this out long ago.'

Ruby swallowed most of the wine and I topped up the glass. She took a bite of her sandwich.

'Yeah, yeah, well I have to hire the kid a maths tutor from the coaching joint in Riley Street. Not cheap, I can tell you.'

I raised my glass to her.

'Ruby, darling, he's lucky to have a granny like you.'

'Right. And just think how useful it'll be to have a bloody doctor in the family.'

Just a chance remark but, after Ruby made short work of the meal, I reflected that a tutor would be one-on-one with a pupil for at least an hour at least once a week, maybe more. And possibly for a fairly long period, if the need was great. Money wouldn't have been a problem. Who better to know things other people might not know?

Fonteyn's list showed that Juliana's tutor was Ambrose Hastings. A landline and a mobile number were given for him. I checked the white pages and found he lived in Bondi. I couldn't see Juliana riding her bike from Vaucluse to Bondi so Hastings must have done his tutoring at the house. Even better; that would give him access to the brother, stepmother and the servants and, possibly, the girl's room. Then again they might have done their work by the pool or in the games room or the gym, which I was sure would be in the house somewhere. I imagined a billiards table, card-playing set-up, a dartboard, a rower and other exercise machines—things we all need.

It was 3.00 pm on a Friday. What does a maths tutor do on Friday arvo? I had no idea. I rang the mobile.

'Hastings.'

'Mr Hastings, my name's Hardy. I'm a private investigator hired by Gerard Fonteyn to look into the disappearance of his daughter. You could call him to . . .'

'No need, I've been through this before. You want to talk to me, I suppose.'

'I do, if you could tell me where and when.'

'Well ... I must say that's better than some of the summonses I've had. I'm at home in ... *Bondi* after a rather hard week. You could come here and I could give you some time, I suppose.'

He gave me the address I already had—a flat in a street a few blocks from Campbell Parade—and I said I'd be there within the hour. Easy. Too easy? There was something about the contact that irked me. Was it the voice? Rounded vowels, private school, or the manner—a been-there-done-that world-weary tone. I puzzled about it on the drive and located my concern just as I bluffed someone out of a parking space near the flat. I'd posed as a stagehand when I'd investigated a theft within a theatre company and I'd worked on films as a bodyguard and armourer. Ambrose Hastings might have been a maths tutor, but the pauses, the amplitude, the emphases, marked him as an actor. When they do it on stage or for the cameras for long enough it rubs off on them.

Nothing is cheap in Bondi these days, but Hastings's block of flats would have to qualify as very downmarket. A small building housing only four flats, it was poorly maintained with the brickwork acned by the salt air and the paint peeling on the wood around the windows. Cement everywhere and the worst feature of all in that area—no parking spaces for the residents. If Hastings had given up acting, notoriously hard to make a living at, he wasn't doing much better as a tutor.

Basic intercom security. I buzzed number four and heard the trained voice again.

'Hardy?'

'Yes.'

'Come up.'

The door release clicked. I went up a flight of concrete steps to the level above and knocked on number four. It opened. The man in the doorway was medium-sized, say 180 centimetres give or take; his dark hair had a pronounced widow's peak and he sported a close-cropped goatee. He wore a short-sleeved white shirt outside loose grey trousers, sandals. He ushered me in and we shook hands.

'Bloody *hot* box, this beastly flat,' he said. 'Come and sit by the fan. There's also a bit of a view, which is the place's only attribute.'

We went down a short passage into a small living room where a couple of armchairs were drawn up near a coffee table under a decent-sized window. The view was over low-rise buildings to the water with just a glimpse of the rocks to the north. A fan was whirring overhead.

Hastings pointed to a chair. 'That's the least uncomfortable. Would you prefer white wine or beer? I've nothing harder.'

25

He made it sound like a line from a play where one character is feeling out the possible weakness of another. Two can play at that game.

'Thanks,' I said, 'whatever you're having.'

'Right, let's be chummy.'

I looked around the room. The other furniture consisted of a dining table with four chairs, a low bookcase and a cabinet holding a TV and DVD player, all shabby like the carpet. The cream-painted walls had faded to a dingy off-white and the only feature of the room that appeared to be well-tended was the scrupulously clean window. Hastings clearly preferred looking out to looking in. There was one muddy painting on a wall well away from the window. I sat down.

Hastings returned with a bottle of Jacob's Creek riesling in an ice bucket. And two glasses.

'Stuff heats up fast in here; doesn't matter so much with good wine but it's *death* to the cheaper stuff. Ever notice that?'

'I don't drink enough good wine to know the difference.'

His laugh surprised me; it was genuine, not stagey. 'Neither do I these days.'

He poured the glasses two-thirds full and nestled the bottle back in the ice.

'Cheers,' he said. 'And what can I do for you?'

I gave it to him straight, saying that I was still undecided about accepting the case and looking for anything to refute the police view.

'Which is what?' Hastings said with raised eyebrows.

I had no compunction in telling him what Cartwright had concluded and giving my opinion that it had affected the investigation by others.

'That's ridiculous,' Hastings said, 'but hardly surprising. The cop I spoke to couldn't conceal his envy of Fonteyn and his consequent dislike of him. Sheer prejudice. I hope you don't share it. Fonteyn is a brilliant man who made the most of his talent. I suppose he had some luck, which is a random thing. Some have it, some don't.'

He was clearly talking about himself and I let him talk as we worked our way through the wine. He said that Juliana had no flair for maths or physics but enough native intelligence to be able to reach what he called a competence.

'She was a *charming* girl, very natural and unassuming despite her talents being in other directions and her manifest advantages. She treated me with respect, as did her father.'

'What about the stepmother?'

He shook his head. 'I never laid eyes on her. I gather she led a very active social life.'

'Did you notice any change in Juliana's behaviour in the time leading up to her disappearance? Her father said she became moody and bad-tempered.'

He thought for a moment. 'No, I can't say I did. But— teenagers! They can be absolute *hell-hounds* at home and nice as pie when they're out.'

27

He'd had three glasses to my one and a bit and it was having an effect. He frowned, fidgeted and stared out the window.

'Mr Hastings,' I said. 'You must've spent quite a bit of time with Juliana and at the house. With all the publicity you must have thought about it. Do you have a theory about what happened to her?'

He jerked himself out of his reverie and poured the last of the wine into his own glass.

'I most certainly do. I think the brother killed her and probably raped her as well. Him and his poxy friend.'

4

Hastings enjoyed my startled reaction. But I was thinking that the attitude change Fonteyn had described could be a result of being abused by her brother. If it had happened.

'He's a vicious little brute,' Hastings said. 'I believe he hated his sister and his father and his stepmother. Hated everybody, I suspect.'

'Including you?'

'Especially me. As you may have gathered, I've fallen on hard times. That painting you looked at is a McCubbin. It's worth quite a lot of money but I hang on to it as a last shred of . . . well, never mind. I'm a failed academic and a failure at quite a few other things. I eke out a living as a tutor and this crummy place is all I can afford. My clothes are shabby despite my best efforts to keep up some front. "Foxy" Fonteyn took me in at a glance and treated me like shit on his shoe from the first.'

'Foxy?'

'What I heard one of his pals call him once. It fitted his appearance and his personality and I've thought of him as Foxy ever since. I understand Americans have another meaning for the word but, as Evelyn Waugh said, they don't really have anything very interesting to say, do they? Have you read Waugh?'

'No. I saw *Brideshead* on TV.'

'Brilliant man. Great writer. I was in a couple of plays . . . never mind. Anyway, you asked and I've told you. I'm afraid I'm out of wine.'

I stood. 'That's all right. You've been very hospitable and helpful.'

He looked at me blankly. 'Have I?'

'Just a few more questions. Did you share your suspicions about Foster Fonteyn with the police?'

'I most certainly did.'

I mulled this over, thinking how it tied in with Cartwright's assessment of the son's hostility.

'You saw a good deal of the boy, then?'

'God no, as little as possible, but I heard him raging about, using filthy language about everybody in his family and others. A companion whose name I don't know and don't want to know was egging him on. Drugs involved, no doubt.'

'Apart from your dislike of the boy and his mates did you have any other grounds for thinking he was involved?'

'Juliana complained about him going into her room and messing with her belongings.'

'Messing how?'

'Trying on her clothes, for all I know.'

'D'you think he was that way inclined?'

'There's no way to tell, is there? I just mean that as well as being foully abusive he's also secretive, *sly*. He found out about some of the wretched films and television disasters I was in and would call me Olivier, O'Toole and the like.'

'Where did you conduct your lessons?'

'In a room set aside for the purpose, why?'

I knew he was holding something back and I decided it was time to put a needle in. 'Not in Juliana's room?'

'You're being offensive.'

'I have to be. I need to know how close . . .'

'I think that's enough. A lost pupil represents a drop in income for me, nothing more. A significant drop, in this case. Perhaps someone in your line of business can understand that.'

He wasn't acting now; he was genuinely affronted and worried about his future. He shot the painting a look that could only be described as despairing. I was tempted to apologise but I didn't. When you start apologising for raw edges in my business it's time to quit. I thanked him again but he was sunk in depression and anger and ignored me. He'd probably try to relieve it with more wine. *Good luck with that*, I thought.

*

The following week I interviewed the Fonteyns' servants, several schoolteachers, her tennis and swimming coaches and the brother and stepmother. The servants spoke highly of the girl and expressed regret about her disappearance and the effect it had had on their employer. The coaches, who used the facilities at the school by special arrangement, both said that Juliana had a high level of natural ability and a reasonable work ethic but not the sort of motivation that would project her beyond the ranks of the gifted amateur. It sounded just like what Sergeant Casey Prescott, the boxing coach at the Maroubra Police Citizens Boys' Club had said of my boxing and 'Salty' Lewis at the Surf Life Saving Club had said of my surfing.

Juliana had been collected by her father following the after-school sessions, but according to the coaches, he'd displayed none of the sort of passion exhibited by parents trying to live vicariously through their kids' achievements. He'd paid generously, taken an interest, watched attentively and was encouraging, and that was all.

The stepmother, Sonja Fonteyn, was one of the most peculiar people I'd ever met. A rail-thin, ethereal ash-blonde, she was such a combination of affectations, pretensions and fragilities that I found it hard to put realistic questions to her. When I did, her replies baffled me. She received me in the Vaucluse house's drawing room, where she floated around, touching objects as if she was afraid they'd disappear, chain-smoking and arranging her elegantly dressed body in seductive postures which lasted for only seconds.

Foster Fonteyn was hard to track down. He was living at home in theory but, having a gap year before deciding which university to attend and what course to take, he was seldom there. I left messages on his mobile that he ignored. Eventually the gardener told me where he often hung out—at a Double Bay wine bar for the well-heeled, where, as I found out after two unsuccessful visits, a glass of wine cost ten bucks. And not a generous glass either. On my third visit he was there, easily recognisable from photographs his father had given me and from Hastings's description of him. He was short, thin, and without anything of Fonteyn Senior's presence. His narrow face with close-set eyes, long nose and thin mouth did indeed give him a foxy look.

He bought a glass of white and slid into a booth. I plonked myself down beside him.

'Hey,' he said.

I showed him my licence and he groaned. His eyes were red-rimmed and there was a strong smell of marijuana on his breath when he spoke.

'Not another fucking one.'

'I'm afraid so, Foxy. Nice to meet you after all this time.'

He shifted as if to push me aside but he didn't have the heft or the real resolve. He was very pale and dressed too warmly for the day in a leather jacket. His hands shook as he picked up his glass and I wondered if grass was the only drug he was on.

'I don't know what happened,' he said. 'I've said it a hundred times.'

'Do you care?'

'Of course I fucking care. Leave me alone.'

'I know someone who thinks you killed her.'

There was a pause, almost imperceptible, but a pause. 'I didn't.'

I persisted. I didn't like bullying a half-stoned kid but this was one of my last shots and I had to give it a go. His answers were monosyllabic mumbles. At one point I deliberately jolted his elbow so that he spilled his wine. I wanted to see how he reacted but he seemed not to care. I gave up, bought him another glass of wine, warned him not to drive and left.

Dr Anna Rosen, the psychologist who'd seen Fonteyn as an obsessed fantasist, had taken up an appointment at MIT. I emailed her but got no reply. It wasn't likely that she'd discuss a case at a distance, if at all.

That decided me. It went against the grain to bail out of something so important and interesting but I had no alternative. I had a living to make and that meant turning my attention to matters much less significant and involving. I rang Fonteyn.

'I'm sorry, Mr Fonteyn,' I said. 'I can't see a way forward. I'll send you my account.'

His voice was sad, filled with resignation.

'Yes. I suppose you talked to that thick policeman who thinks I killed my daughter and to that desiccated tutor who thinks my son killed her.'

'I did.'

'And to the teachers and others who all told you what a good person she was and gave you nothing to work with.'

'That's right and so . . .'

'And to my wife, who at least believes Juliana is still alive because a clairvoyant she trusts told her so.'

'Mr Fonteyn, if I persisted, all I'd be doing is wasting my time and your money.'

'Understood. Thank you for your efforts, Mr Hardy. I'll await your account and I assure you it will be promptly paid.'

It was. And that was it until nearly eight months later when I got a phone call from him.

'Hardy,' he said in a voice totally unlike the one I'd last heard. 'I want to re-engage you. There's been a sighting of Juliana.'

5

I almost dropped the phone. 'When? Where?'

'The right questions, of course. On Norfolk Island, of all places. I want you to go there and . . .'

'Hold on. How did this information come to you?'

'A letter with a photo, along with a message saying that the person who made the sighting will explain everything for a payment of ten thousand dollars.'

'Mr Fonteyn, it sounds like . . .'

'No. No, I'm sure it's genuine. You'll agree when you see the photo. She looks older, just as you'd expect, and . . .'

'Photographs can be faked. Touched up, manipulated in all sorts of ways.'

His excitement had almost given way to anger. 'Don't you think I know that? I tell you it's real. She's on the jetty at Cascade Bay in Norfolk, which is a place I've been to. I recognise the backdrop, and the way she's standing is completely characteristic, but I know there's never been a photo of her in quite that pose or in those clothes. Never! I'll scan everything and send it to you.'

He was too emphatic to argue with directly so I asked him why he didn't go to Norfolk Island himself.

'I would, like a shot, but I have a medical problem. Incipient blockages in my lower legs. I can't fly, can't risk the changes in air pressure. They're worried about clots generally. A rogue clot could kill me. You can name your price, Mr Hardy. The way you behaved earlier has given me complete trust in you.'

When a multi-millionaire tells you something like that you listen. He told me that the photo and the message, which had been posted from Norfolk Island a few days ago, instructed him to come to a guesthouse in the island's main town with the money.

'Did this person have a name?' I asked.

When I spoke I heard him draw a relieved breath and got an apologetic but still forceful response. 'I know I shouldn't assume that you can just drop everything. I . . .'

'It's all right,' I said. 'I have to say I still don't think it's likely, but if you're determined to pursue it I'm pleased to help on the same terms as before.'

'Thank you, but not on the same terms. I'll do you an EFT for twenty thousand dollars to draw on for operational expenses. You'll make an assessment of the credibility of the person you contact and I'll trust your judgement.'

'You'll go that far?'

Now the commanding Oxbridge voice sounded tired. 'You know, I sometimes think trust is one of the most important words in the language. Trust in yourself. Mistrust in yourself, trust in others and mistrust in them. We operate according to it.'

'I'll think that over,' I said. 'You still haven't told me the name of the contact.'

'Colin Campbell. It sounds genuine.'

That was a statement made out of hope more than anything else and didn't require a considered response.

'Let's hope so,' I said. 'But I'm not clear about what you'll be paying for. Is it the recovery of your daughter, or just information?'

'I'll pay for confirmation that she was alive at some time after she went missing and information that could lead to her present whereabouts.'

'That's a lot of money for not very much.'

'I've learned not to pitch my expectations too high, and actually it's for quite a lot. It would confirm that neither Foster nor I were involved in her disappearance. Unfortunately it would also confirm Sonja in her fantasies, but that can't be helped.'

This was a man who thought things through. I had other questions but I decided to leave it there.

The photo and the message reached my computer almost immediately. The girl was standing on a jetty that seemed to be more of a breakwater than anything else; very rocky, with the characteristic tall pine trees in the background. She was wearing jeans, sneakers and a T-shirt that all looked like Kmart. Facially, she resembled Juliana Fonteyn very closely but she appeared to have put on weight. She also appeared to be unaware of the photo being taken because her gesture—pointing down at something in the water—was completely unstudied. I saw what Fonteyn had meant by her action being characteristic of her. Juliana was left-handed and this person was pointing with her left hand.

Digital photos are easy to fake, as I'd told her father; nothing could be simpler than to instruct someone to look like and act like a leftie. But I had to agree with Fonteyn, there was something convincing about the image. I studied the picture through a magnifying glass; Juliana had an olive tint to her skin and, living where she did and given her activities, she was likely to have been tanned when she went missing. But this girl was a few shades darker than I'd have expected, as if she'd been out in the weather rather than hopping around a tennis court and jumping in and out of swimming pools.

I let my mind run on those lines . . . an island, a jetty, weather-effects; it all added up to one thing—boats. In all the theories there'd been about her disappearance, had anyone suggested that Juliana could have been picked up by a boat sailing past her little private beach? I didn't think so. It was thin as a speculation and perhaps I was just trying to convince myself, but I'd gone in to bat on less evidence and less of a gut feeling before.

The brief instruction was word-processed and the signature above the printed name was illegible. It would be, wouldn't it?

I googled Norfolk Island and mugged up on its turbulent history and present circumstances. The murder of Janelle Patton and, unrelated to that, the prosecution of some residents for sexual offences had had an effect on tourism and the populace, it seemed. It was a place with deep undercurrents and surface tensions.

I called up images of Cascade Bay, confirming that the photograph had been taken there unless some very skilful manipulation had been at play. The Seafarer guesthouse in Kingston appeared to be a three-star establishment at the eastern edge of the town, with basic amenities and boasting informality and good views. Just my sort of place. I sent an email requesting a room and got a confirmation within thirty minutes. Then I booked an early morning flight to Norfolk the next day.

I also googled the name Colin Campbell, as I was sure Fonteyn would have done, and saw why he hadn't mentioned doing it—there were more than a dozen people of that name following all sorts of occupations. There was no way to single one out.

*

I spent the evening in Newtown with my daughter Megan, her partner Hank Bachelor, and Ben and Jack, my two grandsons. I read Jack to sleep with Dr Seuss and then prepared myself to face Ben, who was training for a job with the Spanish Inquisition. His first question was a feint.

'Can you take me to a movie tomorrow, Cliff?'

'What about school?'

Megan rolled her eyes, knowing what was coming. 'Holidays,' she said.

'I'm sorry, mate,' I said. 'I'm catching a flight out first thing tomorrow.'

'Where're you going?'

'To Norfolk Island.'

'Where's that?'

'Out in the Pacific Ocean, but not too far.'

'What's it like, this island?'

I gave him a rundown on the place with a brief and no doubt inaccurate account of its convict history and its relation to the *Bounty* mutiny.

The kid was an information vacuum cleaner. He absorbed this and pondered it. 'Why are you going there?'

'A job, mate.'

'What kind of a job?'

Hank came to my rescue. 'That's enough, Ben. Cliff's jobs are his business. He might tell you something about it when he comes back. Right, Cliff?'

'Right. And I'll bring you back something, you and Jack.'

'Different things, please. He's a baby.'

I took out my notebook and a pen and pretended to scribble. 'Something different. Got it.'

6

Although Norfolk Island's an Australian territory, all Australians need a valid passport to come and go and a baggage check is made. It's not as rigorous as actual overseas travel but it's irritating enough and adds to the annoyance of the stupid instruction not to make jokes about terrorism when you step inside the airport. To my mind, if terrorists rob us of our sense of humour they're really winning.

I went business class on Fonteyn's dime and passed the time comfortably with a light meal, a couple of drinks and Robert Macklin's *Dark Paradise*, a history of the island, which I'd picked up at the airport. Good read. I had my usual travelling companion, a volume of Somerset Maugham's short stories, in my bag as backup, but it stayed there.

Feeling more like an interstate trip, the flight was uneventful and it felt much the same on arrival, though with a touch of time travel—stepping back a decade or three to a more basic set of arrangements and more casual attitudes. I had no idea how long I'd be on Norfolk or where I might go, other than to Cascade Bay, but I hired a Mitsubishi 4WD to get me into Kingston and give me freedom of movement. I checked into the Seafarer and was given a room on the second level. It had all I needed—a toilet, a shower, a ceiling fan and a mini-bar.

I knew that the climate was benign, seldom very hot—even more rarely, very cold. I was prepared, with light clothing and casual shoes. Wearing drill trousers, a short-sleeved shirt and canvas loafers without socks, I walked into the town. It was warm in the late morning and the humidity was high but I didn't need to acclimatise. Early October in Sydney under global warming was much the same.

There were only two banks—Westpac and the Common-wealth. I had long-standing issues with the Commonwealth for its arrogance and intransigence and St George, which was part of the Westpac system, held my mortgage. It wouldn't do any harm for the bank to register that I had dollars to play with, however briefly.

'Will I be able to withdraw ten thousand dollars in cash?'

The female clerk looked alarmed. 'I'll have to check, sir.'

A few minutes later she returned. 'The money can be issued to you in forty-eight hours on the presentation of your card and ID.'

'Thanks.'

'You're welcome. Have a nice day.'

I nodded and left. I had the feeling that she watched me all the way, maybe thinking I was some kind of high roller, although as far as I knew there was no casino in town. I hoped it had made her day.

I spent some time walking around the town to familiarise myself with the place—where to eat and drink, where money was and where it wasn't, and when to be friendly and when to be businesslike. From long habit, I located the police station, hoping I wouldn't have to have anything to do with it.

By late afternoon it was time to go back to the Seafarer and make contact with Colin Campbell—if that was his real name, which I doubted. There was certainly no C Campbell in the local telephone directory, but with so many people only using mobiles that didn't necessarily mean anything.

'Do you have a Mr Colin Campbell staying here?' I asked the receptionist.

The place was half-occupied at best and she didn't need to check.

'No, sir. There's a Mr Colin Cameron.'

I snapped my fingers. 'That'll be him.'

'He's in room nine, just along the balcony from your room.'

'Is he in at the moment?'

'I believe he's in the garden. He's a keen photographer and he seems to find things to interest him there.'

'Thanks, I'll look him up later.'

Getting into room nine was child's play. It was a duplicate of mine and the occupant had put his bag where I'd put mine and distributed his things in much the same way. To judge by the clothes, he was about my height but heavier. Not a book reader; a newspaper and magazine man. Not a smoker but definitely a drinker. There was extra wine in the fridge and a bottle of scotch on a shelf. His passport identified him as Christopher Colin Cameron, born in London forty-four years ago. I was wrong about his height; at 189 centimetres I had three centimetres on him. Hair and complexion fair, very English looking.

A couple of cameras, photographic equipment and a folio of published work certified him as a freelance photo-journalist—perhaps, judging by the dates on the pieces, not doing as well lately as he had in years gone by.

The shadows were forming. I turned on just one light, made myself a generous scotch and ice from his Dewar's and settled into a comfortable chair to wait.

He came in, T-shirt and shorts, camera around the neck, a bit sweaty, heading straight for the fridge. He stopped dead when he saw me.

I lifted my glass. 'Don't say, "Who the hell are you?" or you'll make me think we're in a film. You must have a pretty good idea who I am.'

His accent when he replied was southern English, not top-drawer but not working class. The sort you hear from English actors on television, which I've heard described as 'mockney'.

'From Fonteyn.'

'Right. Why the pseudonym?'

'I'm quite well known in some quarters. I just wanted to keep my identity hidden until I saw what happened.'

He opened the fridge, took out a stubby of beer, twisted off the top and swigged it. He was flabby with a double chin getting underway. The passport photo dated back a while. With the bottle half empty he slumped into a chair.

'Have you come here to hurt me?'

I couldn't resist the cue. 'No, Mr Cameron, I've come here to pay you money, if I think you deserve it.'

'I'm not a blackmailer. I made no threats.'

'True, and I'm not hired muscle. I'm a private detective working for Gerard Fonteyn, investigating the disappearance of his daughter.' I showed him my licence and Fonteyn's business card. I also showed him the printout I'd made of my account balance, with the recent deposit of twenty thousand dollars, and told him it was a retainer from Fonteyn. I wanted him relaxed, at least for now. But it all had the wrong effect. He finished his beer, unhooked his camera and placed it carefully on the bed. Then he made himself a scotch with ice and a few drops of soda before sitting again and crossing his freckled legs.

'And you feel free to break into my room and look through my belongings, possibly to steal things?'

I waggled the printout at him. 'Get off your high horse, mate. I'm authorised to pay you or tell you to fuck off.'

He got up and turned on the ceiling fan. With the sun gone the room seemed to get hotter. He sat and worked on his drink.

'Yes, that would seem to give you the upper hand. But Gerard is clearly desperate. I've no idea what your rates are—steep I imagine from your attitude—but hiring you and sending you here and so on is a sign of that.'

'Not really,' I said. 'The man is so rich he could hire me for a year and put me up in New York and not feel the pinch.'

'I see. I had no idea. These plutocrats are very good at hiding their wealth. I should have asked for more.'

'You're looking at a whole lot less until you start providing some information.'

'The printout shows a deposit of twenty grand.'

I shrugged. 'Ten of it's for me. I get it whatever happens. It's your ten that's on the line and I think you need it, Col.' I pointed to his folio, which I'd left on the bed. 'Been a while since you did a big money shoot.'

'True, very perceptive of you. What was your name again?'

An old trick to win a point but I let him have it because I could see that his brain was working overtime and I wanted to know the results. 'Cliff Hardy.'

He smiled, showing yellowed teeth. An ex-smoker. I'd wondered why the ashtray from the table on the balcony had been tucked away somewhere.

'It sounds like an assumed name to fit your profession.'

'It isn't. Let's stop the bullshit and get down to business.'

He leaned forward and studied me. He touched his eyebrows and ran a finger down the centre of his chest. I realised that my shirt was open enough to show the top of my bypass scar.

'I'm betting that's not the only scar you have.'

'What's your point?'

'I'm wondering how tough you really are.'

'I don't advise you to find out.'

'Quite. And it's more important to know how smart you are. You see, I lied when I said I didn't know how rich Gerard Fonteyn really is and I did expect an intermediary, though not exactly someone like you.'

He was suddenly sounding very sure of himself. I nodded, waiting to hear why he thought he had my measure.

'This was just the bait, Mr Hardy.'

7

Controlling situations or trying to is my forte, but I felt this one slipping away. Cameron refreshed his own glass and mine and sat back, after making sure his camera was secure on the bed.

'I propose that we work together,' he said.

'At what?'

'This was a very high-profile case in Australia, right? It even went a bit global.'

'I suppose so.'

'Now here I am with some information and here you are like a bloodhound on the scent. Now I know you'll pay me for the information I have and you'll pay my . . . informant too, but that's not my priority. I want to do a deal with you.'

'Unlikely, but try me.'

'I'm on my uppers, more or less, and I'm stuck here. I've got a return ticket to New Zealand but I don't want to go there for reasons I'll keep to myself. I want a ticket out of here and a guarantee of an interview with the girl if everything turns out well.'

'I can't guarantee that.'

'No deal, no info.'

'Only Fonteyn could okay that and I don't think he would.'

'He would if that's my condition for telling you what I know. I'm not a fool, Hardy. A chance like this comes along very rarely. I have to make the best of it.'

I drank some whisky and thought about it. 'Are you sure what you know can lead somewhere?'

'You're fishing and I shouldn't answer, but yes, I'm sure.'

'If you're thinking about the reward, forget it. I asked Fonteyn to let it be known that it's been withdrawn.'

This was true but it didn't faze him.

'I don't care about the reward. I care about my professional reputation and my future. I'll make it easy for you. Hold off on the ten thousand until you get a result. No result, no money. You just meet my expenses until we get to Australia and then come through on the interview.'

'So we're looking to Australia?'

'That was a slip on my part, but yes.'

'You're pretty sure your information's that reliable.'

'I'm gambling on it and I'm gambling on you. You've shown a bit of dash so far and, staking you as he has, Fonteyn must think you're the goods.'

'I'll think about it.'

'My offer could lapse, or be directed elsewhere.'

That was obviously a bluff, but I decided I needed to spend some more time with him to weigh him up. There was a chance he was an experienced con man. It's hard to tell from a brief meeting. Without responding to his proposition one way or another, I surprised him by suggesting we have dinner together for further discussion.

'On me,' I said, 'at a place of your choosing.'

'On Moneybags Fonteyn in fact.'

'If you like.'

'There are a couple of good places, rather pricey.'

I shrugged.

'Give me time to shower and change.'

I felt I'd gained some ground. I finished my drink. 'Bring your camera,' I said.

The restaurant was walking distance away, attached to one of the hotels. It was air-conditioned, white tableclothed, with muted music and skilled waiters—the kind who left you alone but were there the second you wanted them. It was half full. Clearly it was foreign territory to Cameron, whose regular eating places would be further down the scale. We'd both had two solid whiskies, then a shower and a short walk. It'd be interesting to see how he handled the alcohol from here on.

We got a table for two away from the other diners

at my insistence. Cameron wore a white business shirt tucked into grey slacks. Black slip-on shoes. He didn't bring his camera. I stuck with my drill trousers and canvas boat shoes but had a long-sleeved shirt—sleeves casually rolled up.

The menu was extensive rather than adventurous. Cameron ordered quail with rosemary, garlic and red wine sauce for a starter and barramundi as a main. I went for whitebait and swordfish. He ordered a Heineken to wash down his little birds. We shared a bottle of Clare Valley riesling I'd vaguely heard of.

'Cheers,' he said, tapping the elegantly shaped beer stein against my wine glass. 'To a happy collaboration.'

'Maybe. When I find out a bit more about you.'

Over the food and the wine, both of which were good and well served, Cameron told me that he'd been born in Wimbledon, had been to grammar school and studied photography at a polytechnic. He said he was divorced with no children and that digital photography had knocked the stuffing out of photo-journalism.

'They don't want well-researched, carefully photographed material anymore. They'll print stuff taken on mobile phones as if it was professional material. The old editors are spinning in their graves.'

I had a certain amount of sympathy for this line. The private inquiry business had been corporatised and computerised into something entirely different from the way it used to be. I said something of the sort to Cameron, but he shook his head.

'Not the same thing. The print media's fucked. It pays peanuts and the online mags use junk, full of happy snaps.'

I was sure there were a lot of sour grapes in this. I didn't know about online publications, but I knew *National Geographic* and some travel and sports magazines published quality photographs. Some of the evidence was in his room. I must've looked sceptical because he waved his fork with the last chunk of his fish on it and swore when the forkful fell into his lap. He was a sloppy eater and the tablecloth was spattered.

'Not the same. Look at you, getting ten grand or more for a job. The last time I earned money like that . . . fuck it, what about some pud?'

'I'll settle for coffee. You go ahead.'

He pushed the dessert menu away.

'Better not. We might have to do some walking tomorrow.'

'Walking?'

'Yes. Are we going to get down to tintacks?'

'Not now,' I said. 'We're going to go back to the guesthouse and you're going to talk and I'm going to record every word you say. If I'm satisfied with what I hear I'll let you know whether I'll take you on or handle you in another way.'

His pinkish face flushed a deeper shade than before. He seemed to be about to protest but the bill arrived and he leaned forward and saw the total. I laid an Amex card on the docket and he sat back and said nothing.

We settled ourselves on the balcony between our two rooms with a citronella candle burning against the mosquitoes. Cameron with a mug of tea and me with more coffee. I switched on my recorder.

'I was on the jetty at Cascade Bay taking pictures. Freighters have to anchor a kilometre offshore because the water is treacherous and the coast is so rocky, and the cargo comes on lighters pulled by cables. I thought it might make an interesting story. Same for yachts; people wanting to just stretch their legs or who have business to do there come in by rowboat or outboard. I saw this boat, rowed very expertly by a woman, come through the breakers and head for the jetty.

'She tied up and climbed onto the jetty and sort of stretched and pointed at something and that's when I took the picture you've seen.'

'Because she was so good looking,' I said, 'not because she fitted into some scheme that occurred to you?'

'Fuck you. No, I'm not that fast a thinker. Yes, she was incredibly good looking but I'm not a cradle snatcher. Too many people in my game have got into trouble that way. Something about her clicked in my memory. I didn't know what it was but I wanted her picture. I hung around and she got into conversation with a guy who was the only person on the jetty not working—a fisherman or something. I've got bloody good hearing. She said she was from a yacht called the *Zaca 3* and she'd rowed in because she wanted the exercise and thought there might be somewhere to swim. The local told her there wasn't anywhere to swim and she used an unladylike expression, threw a plastic bag into a rubbish bin, jumped back into her boat and rowed off. It all happened in a couple of minutes.

'As I say, something about the girl struck me but as I turned away and got ready to go, more or less out of the corner of my eye, I saw the fisherman, or whatever he was, take the plastic bag out of the rubbish bin. I headed off to my car and thought about it as I drove back to Kingston. The more I reran it the more what she'd said sounded . . . stagey, rehearsed.'

'I can see where this is going.'

He threw the dregs of his tea over the rail into the garden. 'Who couldn't? I poked around a bit. I've done a few stories on yachties and I knew how to find the right registers. The *Zaca 3*'s owned and skippered by a man named Lance Harris, who bought his way out of a marijuana trafficking charge in Vanuatu a couple of years ago. I got this from a journo here who could tell you more, much more.'

'Could?'

'Could, just as I could. For example, I *could* tell you about the *Zaca*'s next port of call.'

'That's something I could probably find out myself.'

'Take some time, though, and you'll never find the bloke I'm talking about. All we need to do is make a little trip tomorrow and you'll be convinced. That's all I've got to say for now, but there's more. Switch off. Goodnight.'

8

Cameron told me he'd come to Norfolk Island from New Zealand, where he'd been based for the past few years. His coverage of the 2010 Pike River mining disaster had been his last decent commission. He said he'd been 'picking up bits and pieces' since and thought he might be able to organise a feature piece on the writer Colleen McCullough, who had a new book coming out. She'd responded positively but when he'd arrived he learned that she was very ill and she'd died soon after—leaving him, as he put it, 'on the beach'.

I got this the next morning as we made a trip into the interior of the island to visit his journalist contact.

'Why not meet him in town?' I asked.

'His wife won't let him come to town. He's a drunk and she keeps him under house arrest. She's one of those *Bounty* descendants. A very tough customer.'

'How did you meet him?'

'In town. He'd sneaked away and was drinking where I was drinking. He's all right until he gets too sozzled. I've got a few things from the mini-bar in a camera bag just to get him oiled. I trust you'll pay for them.'

'Depends on results,' I said.

The Mitsubishi was handling the hills and the below-average-standard roads easily enough. Every so often a breathtaking view of the land and the sea would sweep by us. We passed a few not very prosperous looking farms and a collection of houses that could have just qualified as a village. After an hour or so we branched off onto a steep dirt road and climbed to a clearing where a log house stood with a backdrop of towering pines. Not far away was a stretch of the Pacific Ocean with some rocky outcrops, producing as dramatic a seascape as you'd ever wish to see.

'How come you know the way here if you met him in town?'

Cameron fussed with a camera and some accessories. 'A relative of his wife's drove him home. She asked me to go along to make sure he didn't throw up all over the upholstery.'

A set of rickety wooden steps led up to the veranda in front of the house. A heavily built, dark-haired woman stood at the top of the steps like a sentinel.

'Who're youse?' she said.

'You remember me, Mrs Blake. I brought Rory home with your cousin a while ago.'

'After getting him pissed.'

'He didn't need any help for that, Missus. Could you tell him I want to see him?'

'Why?'

Her bulk made her virtually impassable; she was just this side of obese in a shapeless cotton dress and her Polynesian ancestry showed in her features. Cameron was not deterred; like me, he was experienced at getting his way with hostile people.

'There's a quid in it for him.'

'How come?'

Cameron hefted one of the bags on a shoulder strap. 'I want him to write something. I'm here to take the pictures.'

She pointed at me. 'Who's he, then?'

'He's the man with the money.'

'I'll get him,' she said. 'Better stay out here. House is a fuckin' mess.'

She turned and went inside.

'Charming woman,' Cameron said.

We climbed up and moved along to where a table and some chairs were set up in a spot to optimise the view. Cameron carefully arranged his bags on the table.

'Her bark's worse than her bite.'

'How about you make that the last cliché of the morning?'

'Don't get shitty, Hardy. You're going to be interested.'

A man came out of the house. He was tall and thin, wearing only a pair of shorts. Barefoot. He had a wildly tangled beard that covered the upper part of his chest. He was deeply tanned and smelled bad.

'Hi, Rory. Remember me? Colin Crawford.'

Rory sat down and pulled the makings and a lighter from his shorts pocket.

'Vaguely,' he said in a surprisingly cultivated voice. 'The bitch said something about money.'

'Mr Hardy here's willing to pay for information.'

'About what?'

'About Lance Harris and the *Zaca 3*.'

'Useful information,' I said. 'My name's Cliff Hardy, Mr Blake. I'm a private detective from Sydney. How're you going?'

'Downhill. How much money?'

'Depends.'

I'd been to the ATM and drawn out a thousand of my own money. I put two hundred dollars on the table. 'That's for your kind hospitality.'

'A smartie,' Blake said. 'Nobody likes a smartie.'

'Come on, Rory. There'll be more. Don't look a gift horse in the mouth.'

Blake gave me his full attention for the first time. 'Have you noticed how he talks in clichés?'

I nodded. 'I've warned him about it.'

Blake smiled, showing discoloured, neglected teeth. 'You crack the whip, do you? Fuck, it's catching, but that's good to know.'

He'd taken a lot of time to make a perfect rollie. He worked on it until he was satisfied and then lit up. He took a deep drag, exhaled and suddenly the pristine, pine-scented air was no more.

Cameron glanced back towards the door, unzipped one of his bags and pulled out a few of the miniature bottles from his mini-bar—a gin, a scotch, a vodka.

Blake lifted a grizzled eyebrow. 'No mixers?'

'Fuck you,' Cameron said. 'Here I am, trying to do you a favour and . . .'

'Take it easy.' Blake screwed the top from the scotch and drank half of it in a gulp. 'I was just having a lend of you, to use an expression.'

I was becoming impatient. 'Let's have fewer expressions and more information.'

Blake had consumed most of the cigarette in a few long drags. He snuffed it out between thumb and forefinger without appearing to feel any pain and put the butt in his pocket. He fiddled with the little scotch bottle instead, seeming to need something to occupy his hands.

'Lance Harris has gone by a few different names in his time.' He winked, letting me see he knew or guessed that Crawford, the name he knew Cameron as, was an assumed one. 'He's done quite a few things—been a soldier of sorts, a journalist, which is where I first ran into him working for the *Pacific Islands Monthly*. Now he's a drug runner.'

Cameron took the top off the vodka and had a swig, glancing at me with a look of satisfaction.

Blake ignored him but drew the gin bottle closer. I'd turned on my recorder in the top pocket of my shirt as soon as Blake appeared. Cameron pulled out a camera and did the things photographers do. Blake drank the rest of the whisky.

'What's this all for?' he said.

'It's just for Cliff's records. He has to report to the man with the real money.'

Blake nodded, apparently unworried by the figure he cut. He seemed eager to talk now. 'Lance, let's call him Lance, sails about here and there providing a service. Mostly gunja, but probably other things too. I heard he did well out of kava at one time when it was fashionable.'

'Is this a one-man operation?'

'Not on your life. Lance always has a female companion aboard the *Zaca 3*.'

'It's a strange name,' I said.

Blake took out his butt, lit it, and opened the gin. He gestured to Cameron. 'Got your photo?'

Cameron took out a photograph, or rather a printed out image. It showed a huge sailing boat with two masts and a lot of sails.

'Jesus,' I said. 'That looks like something from the Sydney to Hobart. You'd need a crew for that.'

Blake chuckled, expelling smoke. 'That's the *Zaca 2*, Errol Flynn's boat. Lance thinks of himself as Errol reincarnated.

In fact I once heard him claim to be his illegitimate son, which is bullshit. You only have to check the dates. Flynn died around 1960 and Lance is only in his late forties at the most.'

'Nineteen fifty-nine for Errol,' Cameron said. 'Aged fifty. A lesson to us all.'

Blake shrugged. 'Whenever. No, Lance's boat's just a ketch, thirty foot or thereabouts. Well fitted out though. He looks a bit like Errol, I must admit; handsome, spivvy moustache, good build on him, too. And behaves like him.'

'How?' I said.

'Terror with the women for one thing. Do you know what David Niven said about Flynn?'

I shook my head.

'He shared a house with him and a couple of other actors. In Malibu, I think, when they were all bachelors gay, in the old sense. Niven said, "You could rely on Errol, he'd always let you down." That's Lance, especially with the women. Bit of a crook, our Errol in his New Guinea days, diddling the natives and so on. Again, a bit like Lance.'

'You've stayed in touch, obviously,' I said.

'I wouldn't say that exactly. A postcard or two perhaps.'

I was sure he was lying but there was really only one question I wanted an answer to at this point. 'So where's he going next?'

'Why?'

'Not your concern.'

'It's the girl, isn't it? I remember Crawfie here saying

something about a girl. I was too pissed then to take much notice.'

'As I say, not your concern. He was here a short while ago. Where would he go next?'

Blake flicked the fag end into the shrubbery and sipped gin. 'Fiji, where he got the kava and the Solomons and the Torres Strait Islands, where there was a market. New Zealand, the Cooks. Who knows?'

'I do,' Cameron said.

I paid Blake another three hundred. He took it without thanks and we left.

'Useful?' Cameron said as we got into the car.

'I suppose. Certainly was for you to get shots of us both for your big story.'

Cameron gave a self-satisfied grin.

'He was lying about not being in contact with Harris,' I said as I drove off.

'That's right. I should be in your game. I did some sniffing around and I learned that our Rory moves a bit of grass himself. Do you know anything about the murder of that young woman here a few years back?'

'Just what was in the papers. I've got a book that deals with it but I haven't got that far yet.'

'Dope was involved. There's quite a few cone-heads on the island, I gather.'

I decided to play Cameron along a little before tackling the question of where the *Zaca 3* was heading. 'While we're talking about lying, what's the reason for the false name?'

He smiled. 'Just a bit of fun and games. I thought I might look over the person who asked about Campbell before I saw him, but you headed me off there. Cameron's the name they know me by at the guesthouse. By the way I pay them by the day in cash. I might ask for a little help there, Cliff.'

'You're getting ahead of yourself. You haven't convinced . . .'

I rounded a bend and swore when I saw a ute slewed across the road with one front wheel in a ditch. Two men were inspecting its front end and talking excitedly.

'Looks like they could use some help,' I said. 'Come on.'

We got out and approached the men, both wearing singlets, shorts and thongs. I was only a metre away when one of them produced a machete and the other a flick knife. I sensed Cameron backing away.

Machete said, 'Wallets and keys and no one gets hurt.'

'Keys are in the car,' I said. I moved right up close so he couldn't swing the machete—and what use is a machete if you can't swing it? I drove the heel of my right hand hard against his nose and felt it collapse. He staggered and dropped the machete. I picked it up and slammed it flat against the side of his head and he went down. Flick Knife didn't know what to do as I came towards him, moving the machete to and fro.

'Throw the knife as far as you can into the bush.'

He did it.

'Pick up your dumb mate and dump him in the tray and get the ute started and park it out of our bloody way.'

He was a big guy but fat and slow and he couldn't take his eyes off the machete as I kept it flickering at him, chest-high. He heaved the other man into the tray, got in the ute and revved it hard so that it bullocked free of the ditch and bucked to a stop at the side of the road, where it stalled.

'That'll do.'

Cameron was standing open-mouthed and shocked, either by the threat or my actions. I clapped him on the shoulder.

'Let's go.'

We drove off. I put the machete on the floor of the car. 'Souvenir,' I said.

Cameron was silent for most of the drive back to Kingston. When the town was in sight he said he needed a drink.

'Me too. And then we'll have a little talk.'

'Yes,' he said. 'Yes, of course.'

9

In a dim, cool bar in the first pub we came to, Cameron and I sat over beers with me paying. It was obvious I was going to be doing a lot of that with him along so it was time for him to convince me of the value of his involvement.

'Okay, let's have it,' I said. 'What else do you know about Harris and specifically where's he going next and how do you know about it?'

'Good questions.'

'Don't bugger me about.'

'All right. For one thing I've met Harris and I know what he looks like. I also know his weakness.'

'Which is what?'

'Women.'

'That doesn't make him unusual.'

'Young women, very young, again like Errol Flynn. Got him into trouble a few times. Ms Fonteyn's what, fifteen?'

'Sixteen now.'

Cameron grinned. 'Getting a bit old for Lance, perhaps.'

'What happens to them when they get too old?'

'No idea. Nothing good, I suspect. He hooks them on something from what I saw.'

'What *did* you see? Where and when?'

'Go easy. Get me another beer while I remember.'

It wasn't a comfortable association. He'd recovered from his shock at the road incident and was in an assertive mood. I knew I'd have to pull him into line again soon, but for now I played along and bought him another drink.

'Now,' I said, 'you and Lance.'

'A restaurant in Auckland, say a couple of years ago. I was doing photographs of a wedding party. Pissy little job, but there you are. I noticed this bloke sitting off to one side taking care not to let himself get in a picture—turning his back, putting his hand up to his face, that kind of thing. We notice stuff like that.'

'And?'

'I was curious. Anyway, the groom, who was as pissed as a fart and unlikely to get it up that night, I reckon, gave me a bottle of champagne when I finished. Good stuff. I took it across to where this bloke was sitting with a chick. You couldn't miss his resemblance to Errol Flynn—the features, the mo, the cigarette in a holder. I forget what name he gave but it wasn't Lance. I put that together after my chat with Rory. The girl was very pretty and very young and either pissed or stoned, probably both.'

'And?'

Cameron shrugged. 'We shared the bubbly and chatted. I forget what about. He mentioned a yacht. The girl mostly giggled.'

'Did you ask him why he avoided being photographed?'

Cameron almost choked on his beer. 'Are you kidding? He was big, about your size, and he had the same look as you, not as battered, but . . . in the eyes.'

'And what's that?'

'Fucking dangerous, the way you were back on the road.'

'I've been thinking about that. D'you reckon Blake could've alerted them?'

'You're a suspicious bastard, aren't you?'

'Always. Don't forget it. Well?'

Cameron scratched his unshaven chin where ginger whiskers were beginning to show. 'Maybe, if they were on their way to buy some dope and had a mobile.'

'All right, Col,' I said. 'Now we get to it. Where's the boat going?'

He sucked in a deep breath, marshalling sobriety after the slug of gin and two schooners, and courage. 'When I have my ticket to Oz in my hand.'

I went to the bank and drew out five thousand. Cameron, tipsy, watched this without comment.

I took him to a travel agent and booked a flight to Sydney

for the day after tomorrow. He said he had an entry permit, which I knew was true because I'd seen the stamp in his passport. I paid in cash. He reached for the ticket but I kept hold of it and we went to a café and ordered coffee. Cameron's confidence had evaporated.

'What's this about?'

I waited until the coffee came. He spooned sugar into his cup while I made a show of packing together one-hundred-dollar notes to the amount of two thousand. I flapped the ticket and the money at him without anyone else seeing.

'The destination of the yacht?' I said.

'Fitzroy Heads, in northern New South Wales.'

'How did you find out?'

He slurped coffee, spilling some. 'Harris went ashore at Kingston. He said he was having trouble with his GPS and radio and he wanted to report his next port of call just in case.'

'Could he have been lying?'

'How would I know? Probably not. Yachties are supposed to notify maritime officers of their schedule. I suppose if they're carrying contraband they don't always do it but if their equipment's dodgy—no point carrying a hundred grand's worth of gunja and going to the bottom with it.'

'How long does it take to sail there from here?'

'I asked the coastguards about that,' he said. 'They said it was hard to say and talked about nautical miles and knots per hour and stuff I didn't understand. All I gathered was that it'd be a week or so, give or take.'

'And when did the *Zaca* leave?'

'Eight days ago.'

I handed him the money. 'Two thousand on account. More to come as things develop, trust me.'

He seemed about to complain but thought better of it.

'Okay.'

'That'll easily handle your bill at the guesthouse, including the mini-bar and other expenses.'

He reached for the ticket again but I kept it away from him. 'The other information about Harris you said you had. Like you said, Col—no info, no ticket.'

'Fuck you, Hardy.'

I made as if to tear the ticket in two.

'All right, all right. The guy I met in Auckland said he had a wife living on the Queensland Gold Coast.'

'Name?'

He shook his head.

I handed him the ticket. He looked at it and swore. 'This is for Thursday; there's a plane out tomorrow.'

I handed him my card. 'When you get to Sydney send me a text or an email telling me how I can get in touch with you if things work out in your favour.'

'What about you?'

'I'm on tomorrow's plane. Don't try to change your flight,

Col. I'll be annoyed if I see you. Give yourself twenty-four hours' holiday, all expenses paid.'

'I don't want a holiday.'

'Yes you do,' I said.

part two

10

I flew back to Sydney not dissatisfied with my progress. While I hadn't actually confirmed that the girl in Cameron's photograph was Juliana, the odds—given the resemblance, the athleticism and the left-handedness—were good. At one point Cameron had told me that she spoke with an educated Australian accent and that her left arm was slightly more developed than her right—a sure sign of a left-handed tennis player; he noticed such things from years of photographing sports people. I remembered that Rod Laver's left arm was like a tree branch.

I felt I had enough of a lead to convince Fonteyn that I should continue. There was one question though that was uncomfortable. How would Harris have induced Juliana to go with him? I thought I might have the answer, but it'd need diplomatic handling and not yet.

I phoned Fonteyn and gave him a sketchy outline of how

things stood. He was excited and agreed to meet me at the airport. If I was given the go-ahead I was on my way north.

I was in the bar reading the Macklin book when Fonteyn arrived. Cameron had been right—marijuana had played a part in the death of Janelle Patton.

Fonteyn bustled up, in a suit but without a tie and with the top buttons of his snowy shirt undone—his version of informal. We shook hands.

'You've done well,' he said.

I shook my head. 'There's a lot to find out still, but I want you to listen to this.'

I produced my voice recorder and paused it. 'Can I get you a drink? It's your money.'

He nodded. 'White wine spritzer, thank you.'

I released the pause button and ambled across to the bar, where I waited longer than I needed to. I glanced back and saw that Fonteyn was leaning forward as if in supplication to the device and oblivious of all else.

I returned with the drinks, mine minus the soda. I turned the recorder off after he'd heard the basic stuff about the girl, the yacht and its skipper. He leaned back and took a swig of his drink.

'And do you know where the yacht went?'

'Fitzroy Heads, if this Cameron, which is his real name, is to be believed.'

'And is he? Did you pay him?'

'Not exactly.'

I explained how Cameron was less interested in the money than in re-establishing his career and that he wanted to score an interview with Juliana. Plus his intention to make a big splash with the story.

Fonteyn sipped his drink but I doubt that he tasted it.

'I suppose that'd be all right, strictly supervised. It would depend on her . . . condition . . . her state of mind. Are you saying that the indications are that she's with this individual willingly?'

'That's the way it looks. The question is, how did he snare her in the first place?'

'Snare? Your informant didn't know?'

'No, but he suggested drugs could be involved. Harris has a reputation for . . . influencing young women that way and involving them in his dealings.'

He received this like a man being told he has cancer, closing his eyes and taking a deep breath. 'So there could be criminal charges against her?'

'It's a side issue for now,' I said. 'With your agreement, I intend to go up north to follow these leads. Cameron will arrive in Sydney tomorrow. I recommend that he be followed and located. He might have further information if what he's told me doesn't quite work out. Or another agenda, say.'

'You don't trust him?'

'Mr Fonteyn, I've been in this business a long time. My reserves of trust ran very thin many years ago.'

He sighed. 'I know what you mean. It's an uncomfortable feeling. I . . . have confidence in you. Can you arrange to keep tabs on this man Cameron?'

'Yes, and I need to ask something of you, too.'

'Money? I . . .'

I shook my head. 'I have plenty of your money. Apart from revoking the reward, please don't do anything at your end. And if that attracts any attention, say nothing.'

He stood, leaving most of his drink.

'I agree. Good luck, Mr Hardy. I'm relying on you and I suspect Juliana is as well.'

He walked stiffly away. He'd gone further towards convincing himself that his daughter was alive than he should and I sensed that he was already planning a defence if trouble loomed for her. I felt the pressure. I drained my glass and Fonteyn's—there's nothing much in an eight-dollar-fifty glass of wine at the Sydney airport.

I phoned Hank Bachelor and arranged for him to follow Cameron when he arrived and see where he put himself. Hank used to work for me, now he was on his own in the security business, doing well but too deskbound the way things are these days and he was happy to get out and about.

I caught an afternoon flight to Ballina. Took a bus into Byron Bay, where I hired another Mitsubishi and drove to Fitzroy Heads. I hadn't been in the area for some years and noticed a lot of changes. A new highway running north with complicated directional pointers and a sense that large stretches of what had been open land were now developed.

Fitzroy Heads, where I'd once holidayed with a girlfriend, had seen some changes too, although with its estuary, seawall bridge across the river and extensive mooring docks it retained something of the old fishing and vacation feel. I checked into the Breakwater Lodge and had a swim in the pool. I hadn't had any serious exercise for a few days and I pushed myself, swimming the short laps until I ached in all the right places. After a hot shower and then a cold one I felt as tuned up as I could expect to be at my age.

I used the motel laundry to wash and dry some of the clothes I'd worn for the last couple of days and felt pretty fresh as I walked the short distance to where the water sparkled and the boats floated. The little artificial harbour had jetties lined with vessels of all kinds while a few others were at moorings in the middle and by the banks of the river. If the *Zaca 3* was there, there was no chance of me spotting it.

The Fitzroy Heads Yacht Club was the obvious place to start. Its building was the usual style, painted white and blue, low-slung, as if trying to look like a boat itself. There was a huge open shed with yachts set up on trestles inside and a slipway running down a ramp to the river. Various nautical types were working in the shed and standing, smoking, arguing and pointing as boats jostled for places at the nearby jetty. A set of weather-stained steps led to the clubhouse facilities, including the bar.

Yachties are law-abiding folk on the whole; they're governed by a lot of rules and regulations and they tend to be good at reading people. There was no point in me pretending to be anything other than what I was. I suppose I could've claimed to be wanting to charter a yacht but my ignorance of what was involved would soon be revealed. In my favour was Rory Blake's assessment of Harris as someone who let people down.

The club showed its age inside as well as out but it had a comfortable, well-used feel with carpet that had been spilled on more than once, tobacco-smoke-stained walls, although there was no smoking now, and a long bar. Tables and chairs were scattered about, mostly to take advantage of the view through the window that composed most of one wall.

The visitors' book required only my name and address and the name of any club I belonged to. I filled it in honestly and nominated the Redgum Gymnasium and Fitness Club; stretching things a bit. There were three men at the bar and perhaps a dozen sitting in twos and threes at the tables. I went up and ordered a middy of Pure Blonde.

The barman, a veteran of the trade, said, 'Getting popular, that.'

I nodded, paid for the drink and jerked my head sideways, indicating I wanted a private word. He pulled the beer and shuffled to the right as if looking for a safe place to deliver it. I put twenty dollars and my licence on the bar.

'I want the drink, all right—I've come a fair way—but I want information more.'

I do a lot of work in pubs where the noise can be deafening at any time of the night or day. It was unusual to be asking questions in a quiet atmosphere with only muted conversation and the occasional laugh providing the backdrop. I forced myself to keep my voice low.

'You look like you belong here,' I said, picking up the licence but leaving the money.

He plucked it from the bar. 'Born and bred, mate.'

'I'm looking for a man who sails a yacht called the *Zaca 3*. I've been told he was due to put in here—is that the expression? By the way, you are . . .?'

'Hector. This a criminal matter?'

'Hard to say.'

'Bullshit. That cunt somehow got credit at the club bottle shop. I suppose the kid in charge was impressed by the yacht and Lance's usual crap. He never paid up and he left owing money here and there. Shit, he was always slippery, but he's gone a bit far this time. He'll be lucky to get another mooring anywhere in this state. The secretary here put the word out.'

'When he was in here was he alone?'

'Mostly.'

'But not always?'

'One time he had a girl with him—real young and pretty pissed. He was asked to leave. That was the last time he was here.'

I produced the photograph.

'That's her,' Hector said. 'Poor thing.'

'When were they here?'

'Ten days, couple of weeks ago?'

'Any idea where he might've gone?'

Hector shrugged and went down the bar to serve another customer. I drank my beer and pondered my next question. I had another twenty for Hector when he returned.

'The last place he was at he said his GPS and radio weren't working properly.'

Hector nodded. 'Had 'em fixed here by an expert. That's where he owes the most money.'

'I'd like to talk to whoever did the work. He might know where Harris was headed.'

'She,' Hector said. 'Old flame of Lance's. That'd be why he put in here—to make use of someone he knows and rob her blind. The nerve of the bastard. Turns up with another bird in tow and does that.'

'What's this woman's name? Where can I find her?'

'Molly Featherstone. She's got a workshop behind the hardware store in the main street. Treat her gently, eh?'

'Why's that?'

'Molly and Lance's chick got into it somewhat, and Molly came off worse.'

'This's not such a small place. How come you know all this?'

'Molly's my niece. If you do ever catch up with Lance, kick the shit out of him for me. You look like you could do it, but be careful, he fights dirty.'

'So do I,' I said.

11

I found the hardware store and the workshop behind it. The roller door was open. I went in and a woman looked up from the bench where she was working. An array of electronic apparatus was spread out in front of her.

She was blonde with frizzy hair, mid-thirties at a guess but hard to tell because of a dressing fixed to the left side of her face. Her right cheekbone carried a fading bruise. She wore a sleeveless denim overall with a white T-shirt under it.

'Ms Featherstone?'

She put down what she was working on. 'Yes.'

I moved past boxes and more gear I didn't recognise until I was up at the bench. I put my licence folder down in a space between the bits and pieces.

'Your uncle Hector suggested I have a talk to you.'

She touched the dressing. 'Talking still hurts a bit. What about?'

'Lance Harris and the woman who was with him.'

'Woman! She's just a girl and a vicious bitch at that. Why're you interested?'

There was a stool off to one side. I pulled it over and sat. 'I'm working for the girl's father. She's a runaway, sort of. What name was she going by?'

'Rich father?'

'Very.'

'Figures. Lance'll find a way to bleed him.'

I picked up the folder. 'Not if I can help it. Tell me what happened.'

'Why should I help her?'

'You'll be helping me put Lance in hospital before he goes to gaol.'

She grinned and then winced as the movement hurt her face. 'I like that. You sure you could do it?'

I nodded.

'Maybe you could, at that. Do you drink instant coffee?'

'When there's nothing better.'

She stood, medium tall and strongly built, and moved to a corner of the workshop where she had an electric jug, a large tin of International Roast and mugs on top of a bar fridge. She boiled the water, spooned in the coffee and offered me milk and sugar. I took both.

She talked for the next twenty minutes, only interrupted by a few questions from me and several phone calls that she handled briskly. She said that Harris had asked her to fix his

GPS and radio and run a check on the *Zaca 3*'s generator. She'd agreed reluctantly because of the sour taste left by their break-up and the presence of the girl, who was introduced as Trudi.

'He paid me a bit up front, so I took the chance,' Molly said.

Harris was in a hurry; Molly did the work quickly and the bill was heavy. She said he was having other things done to the boat but that he seemed to have plenty of money.

'Did you know he was a drug dealer?'

'Sure, grass—someone has to do it.'

She said that when she presented Harris with the account he started to quibble about it, claimed she was over-charging him and had used second-hand materials. She got angry and accused him of trying to welsh on the bill and threw in things about his drug dealing and his liking for young girls.

'Such as?' I said.

'You know—how young girls can't tell the difference between a real lover and an everyday fuck. This Trudi came at me like a bat out of hell. She belted me here,' she touched her cheek, 'and she clawed my face. Dug in bloody deep. I'll say this for her, she's bloody strong for her age.'

'If I can find her I'm pretty sure I can get her father to pay your bill and some compensation.'

'I won't hold my breath. She belongs in a cage. Just put Lance through the wringer and tell him it comes from me.'

'To do that I need to know where he's gone. Does he have to register his next port of call with someone?'

'Should, but what Lance should do and what he bloody does are two different things. The word's out on him along this coast but Queenslanders wouldn't care. The Gold Coast's a zoo. I'd say he's gone to Coolangatta. Easy sail, big market there. He'd have contacts.'

'I'm told he has a wife on the Gold Coast.'

She shrugged. 'That's right.'

'D' you know her name?'

'Deirdre, Drusilla, Diana, something like that. She's a stripper, or she was. Look, to tell you the truth I'm a bit tired of thinking about that bastard.'

'Understood. I'll let you know if there's a prospect of some money. I'm at the Breakwater if you think of anything else.'

'You didn't drink your coffee.'

'Neither did you. It was all too interesting for instant coffee.'

I walked back to the motel as the day cooled and a sea breeze sprang up, promising a pleasant evening for those on boats and on land. A man was leaning on my car outside my room. He wore a well-cut beige lightweight suit, pale blue shirt, no tie, Panama hat. He eased away from the car and opened his hands in a gesture that said no threat. Not a gesture to trust.

'I'd like a word with you,' he said in a voice carrying a faint trace of an accent. Italian? Greek?

89

'And you are . . .?'

He dropped the hands. 'Just someone who happens to know you have an interest in Lance Harris.'

'How would you know that?'

'I was in the sailing club bar and I have very keen hearing.'

I thought back to the scene in the club, the drinkers at the bar, the people at tables, some with their backs to me. It was possible.

'A word, you said. Are you offering to help me find him?'

He took off his hat and smoothed back thick dark hair. He fanned away some insects. 'No. No, I wish I could. I just want you to deliver a message when you do find him.'

'You think I will?'

He nodded. 'I got your name from Hector and checked you out, Mr Hardy. I think you'll find him.'

He was at least ten years younger than me, tall, very fit looking and keeping a calculated distance between us. Now there were a few other people around—guests arriving.

'Okay,' I said. 'What's the message?'

'Just tell him George is disappointed at not getting his delivery.'

'George who?'

He smiled, replaced his hat and moved away quickly in long, relaxed strides. I went into my room and sat down to jot a few notes and think things over. In the space of an hour or two I'd found three people who wished Lance Harris ill. The man had a world-class talent for making enemies.

It had been a long day with a lot of territory covered. I had a beer from the mini-bar and reread one of my favourite Maugham stories—'The Fall of Edward Barnard', about a man who remade himself.

I ate in the restaurant attached to the motel and was just finishing up when Molly Featherstone walked in. She'd shed the overall and was in the white T-shirt and jeans. She came across to my table.

'Hi,' she said.

'Hello.'

'Mind if I talk to you? I feel I was a bit rude earlier on.'

'You weren't, but please sit down. There's a bit of wine left. Would you like some?'

'No thanks. I'm off it. Look, I've come to eat humble pie. You mentioned that there might be some money available and I pooh-poohed it. Well, the fact is that my business is struggling and Lance running out on me has dealt it a body blow. If Trudi's rich dad *is* feeling generous, I'd be grateful for some help.'

'I'll make a point of asking him. I'm sure something can be done. And while you're here, perhaps you can help with something else. A man named George approached me, a tall, well-dressed and -groomed bloke with an accent. He left a message for me to give to Harris if I catch up with him. Do you know who he could be?'

She nodded. 'George D'Amico.'

'What is he? A yacht owner? A businessman?'

'You could say he's a businessman. He owns a couple of brothels up here in the Northern Rivers, and he provides . . . escorts for people going on yacht cruises.'

'So he's a pimp?'

She smiled. 'Yes, although I'm sure he'd have another name for his services. What was the message?'

'Never mind. It makes sense to me now. There's one other thing about Harris—does he read the papers, watch the news, use the Internet?'

'Lance? He's dyslexic. He never reads anything and all he watches on television is porn. He's an IT-primitive except for sailing information.'

'Thanks, that's interesting. Give me your card. I'll contact my client and he'll have someone contact you. Don't hold back with what you ask for, you've been very helpful. I'll advise settlement of your account and an equal amount in compensation for your injury and for your assistance. How'd that be?'

'Fantastic. I can't thank you enough, Mr Hardy.'

'Cliff. Stay afloat, Molly, help is on its way.'

The Breakwater Lodge was quiet—everyone coming in was in and everyone going out was out. The bed was comfortable and the air-conditioning was quiet. I felt I was making progress and, unlike sometimes when I was frustrated and angry and lay awake turning things over in my mind and having disturbing dreams, I slept soundly and late.

I was becoming fond of the Breakwater. I had a leisurely swim and an equally leisurely breakfast, shower and shave so that it was almost mid-morning before I checked out. No complaint from the management about the lateness and I left a tip for whoever cleaned the room—all on Fonteyn.

I filled the tank and pointed myself towards the sunshine state. I hadn't gone more than a kilometre towards the highway when my mobile rang. I pulled over.

'Hardy.'

'Cliff, this is Hank. Sorry, mate, your guy arrived on time and bought himself a ticket. He's sitting in the departure lounge right now. Do you want me to do anything?'

'No. Where's he headed?'

'Ballina. Plane goes in an hour. Is there a problem?'

'No. Thanks, Hank.'

'He socked down a couple before he bought his ticket. He doesn't look like much.'

'He's a softie, but persistent.'

I cut the call and got moving. *Bloody Cameron*, I thought. He'd probably done enough snooping in his time to pick up my trail in Fitzroy Heads and he had the money to follow it. He was well off the pace but a nuisance and just maybe something more.

In a way I was pleased—things had been going too smoothly and I was feeling comfortable, always a bad sign.

12

Since the last election Queensland has recovered some way from the slide towards the police state that had threatened with the previous government. Probably some of the laws that had criminalised people for their associations were still on the books but it looked as though they weren't being enforced as officiously. Still, in a fundamentally conservative territory, things could slip back.

Coolangatta feels artificial and temporary, as if something might easily pack the whole place up and move it away. It boasts sunshine, sand and surf, and money. A good bit of the money is newly arrived and a lot of it is expressed in boats. I drove to the marina, or as close as I could get to it. It was Saturday and it seemed that every car for miles around had come to the city centre and the adjacent attractions like the marina.

I walked in the warming morning to the harbour and let

my eyes drift over the sparkling scene. White predominated—
money afloat, washed clean. Some of the bigger boats had
play areas and gardens on their decks.

Chances of spotting the *Zaca 3* were nil and there were
too many sailing clubs and organisations to make legwork
profitable. I needed local help and I had some in the person
of Vaughan Turnbull, a private investigator who'd helped
me before when I'd been up here chasing a maintenance-
defaulting husband. I drove to the office he had in a low-
rise building several blocks back from where the spray hit
the sand.

Vaughan was a bit younger than me, just enough to be
respectful. He was hungry when I'd last seen him and, unless
the business had taken a turn for the better up here in the
last few years, I guessed that he still was. We single operators
are an informal bunch; I didn't phone ahead. My calling
card was a chilled six-pack of Little Creatures Bright Ale. If
he wasn't in I'd phone him and tell him I had it; if he was,
I'd put it on his desk.

After parking a couple of blocks away and walking in the
sun, the air-conditioning in Vaughan's building was welcome.
The place held a mixture of slightly offbeat businesses
and several vacant suites. One floor up, I pushed open the
unlocked door with *Turnbull Investigations* stencilled on the
glass and went into a small foyer that could've just about held
a secretary, but didn't, and rapped on the door behind it.

'Come in.'

I walked into a fair-sized office containing all the standard equipment of the profession and plonked the six-pack on the desk.

The man sitting there turned away from his computer and faced me.

'Cliff Hardy,' he said. 'The Sydney sleuth. How the fuck are you?'

'Getting along, Vaughan. Want to crack a couple of these?'

'Why not? Have a seat.'

He deftly closed the long blade open on the Swiss Army knife on his desk and unclasped the bottle opener. With the tops off we clinked bottles and Vaughan took a long swig.

'Not bad,' he said. 'But I take it you haven't come just to bring some Sydney sophistication to the deep north.'

'No, I need your help. I've got a paying client and you'll be a legitimate expense.'

Vaughan had aged in the few years since I'd last seen him. Back then he'd been a gymaholic and surfer and about as fit as a man pushing fifty could be. Now he carried more flesh and had more wrinkles, but his hands were steady and his eyes were clear.

He laughed. 'I've been called a few things in my time but that's a newie. What's the job?'

I told him as much as necessary to put him in the picture. He listened intently while sipping on the beer, nodding occasionally, as when I mentioned Hector the barman's claim that the word would be out in New South Wales ports on the *Zaca 3*, and the encounter with George D'Amico.

When I'd finished he said, 'Deirdre or Diana and a stripper, past or present. It's something to start with. I know about George D'Amico. He's got a place up here. The word is he greases the right palms in politics and the constabulary. A man to be very careful of, Cliff.'

'He was issuing a warning to Harris through me. Would he be likely to have someone watching my progress?'

'More than likely.'

'And be looking for Harris himself?'

'Depends on how pissed off he is.'

'He was very smooth, hard to tell.'

'With D'Amico, assume the worst.'

We drank our beer and didn't say anything for a few minutes. Vaughan's office was spick and span, which either meant he was an efficient organiser or didn't have a lot to do.

I broke the silence. 'Drugs, marijuana, possibly other things. If Harris was looking to do business up here, how would he go about it? Assuming he's been operating here before.'

'The scene's changed. The crackdown on the bikies has had some effect, not too much. They're not stupid. You cut your hair and trim your beard, wear a Gold Coast Suns or a Brisbane Broncos shirt and don't rev your Harley too hard and the cops don't react. But the supply's down and some freelancers'll be getting busy among the kids.'

'Any connection with yachties?'

'Fuck you. I was just about to say that some of the well-heeled kids, and believe me there are some, charter boats to cruise about and get drunk and stoned and dip their wicks if they're lucky, out on the water.'

'Sounds like a scene Harris'd enjoy. You must have some contacts, and then there's the wife angle. Have you got anything big on just now?'

He shook his head. 'Nothing that can't wait.'

'We'll have to decide how to divide the work up.'

'Time is money.'

I'd stopped off at a bank on the way to see him, and had a wallet stuffed with Gerard Fonteyn's money. I counted out a thousand dollars in hundreds and put it on the desk.

'Money talks,' Vaughan said.

I had a reservation before we got going.

'Are these lines of investigation going to cross? I mean, strippers, prostitutes . . .'

'No,' Vaughan said. 'D'Amico's places specialise in young girls, as young as he can get away with.'

'Are you sure you're okay with this? It could get sticky.'

'Mate, I'm more than okay. You knew I was divorced?'

I shook my head.

'Oh yeah, after you were last here. She stripped me bare and I don't blame her. I was almost never there and not really there when I was there.'

'I know what you mean.'

'Yeah, well I was down for a while, got on the piss, but I'm back on my feet now. One of my three kids still talks to me. But everything I've got is leased or rented. I want the work and I'll give it my best shot. A grand's a good start but information's expensive in this town.'

I told him there was the prospect of more expense money and a bonus if things worked out and he seemed satisfied.

He told me that while prostitution was legal in Queensland and there were licensed brothels, only a small percentage of sex work went on in them. Otherwise the scene operated in a variety of different ways—individuals in their own premises, pairs in similar set-ups, massage parlours and escort services.

Vaughan went off to try to track down the wife and I went to George D'Amico's establishment. I thought I'd talk to whoever was there to see how serious D'Amico was about wanting the message to get to Harris. And such places can provide information about the drug scene if you ask the right questions of the right people and have the right money.

D'Amico's Classic Escorts was in a free-standing, double-fronted townhouse not far from a cluster of motels and holiday rental apartments—an ideal set-up.

I drove there using the local street map Vaughan had given me and parked the Mitsubishi a block away. I'd debated whether to go to a motel and clean up but decided against it. At that time of the day I had a heavy stubble and my clothes were rumpled, but I wasn't intending to make an impression other than as someone wanting information and resolved to get it.

A high wall surrounded the property and there was provision for underground parking. A gate in the wall was protected by a high-mounted camera and an intercom. I pressed the buzzer.

'Yes?'

A female voice, sceptical. I was being looked at from inside. I held my licence folder up to where a faint glow indicated a camera constantly at work.

'I have a message for George D'Amico.'

'Mr D'Amico isn't here.'

'I know. I saw him in Fitzroy Heads yesterday. I want to talk to whoever is in charge here.'

'Just a moment.'

After a minute or so the door swung open. I went up a short path, through an open door and into a quiet, air-conditioned reception area with a desk, armchairs, coffee tables and photographs of women on the walls. There was no one at the desk although an almost full coffee cup and a half-smoked cigarette with a lipstick mark on the filter stubbed out in an ashtray suggested it had been recently occupied. A man in a light grey suit came down a set of stairs to the right. He noticed my startled reaction and smiled.

'So you have met George. I'm his brother Paul. What can I do for you?'

'Twins?'

'Not quite. Ten months apart. I'm the younger, unfortunately. Could I see that ID again, please.'

I showed him the licence and he examined it carefully. He waved towards some chairs positioned around a low table but I stood my ground.

'This isn't social, Mr D'Amico.'

'I hope not. I'm not in the habit of socialising with scruffy private eyes.'

'I don't think a pimp is in a position to be that choosy. I'm here to talk about Lance Harris and his Lolita.'

That startled him. 'Are you now? I must apologise, Mr Hardy. I think we should have a drink and a talk.'

13

Paul D'Amico conducted me upstairs. Looking back, I glimpsed a woman coming from outside and slipping into the chair by the desk. I could smell the smoke on her.

'Offensive habit,' D'Amico said. 'I discourage it, but it goes with the territory in this kind of establishment.'

I nodded. Like his brother he had a slight accent and moved athletically. Something about the set-up here struck a false note with me but I couldn't put my finger on it. We went into an office better fitted out than mine or Vaughan Turnbull's but not as expensively as Gerard Fonteyn's. He waved me into a chair and opened a bar fridge.

'Scotch? Single malt.'

'Thanks. Small one, neat.'

'"Straight up", as the Yanks say.'

He was turning on the charm and I wasn't buying it.

'I never really knew what that meant. Spend much time there learning the business?'

He prepared the drinks, adding a block of ice to his. He was a man who liked to make a point. Instead of sitting behind the desk he rolled the chair out beside it so that we were face to face, both using the desk as somewhere to place our glasses.

He raised his glass in a gesture I could respond to or not. I didn't.

'So you're on a missing persons case and Harris has her?'

I took a sip of the smooth scotch. I remembered an episode of the TV show *Taggart* in which a Chinese woman praised the calming benefits of meditation. Taggart replied, 'I know a single malt'll do that.' This was the stuff.

'It looks that way.'

'How old?'

'Sixteen by now.'

'Getting on for Lance.'

'So I've been told. And for you.'

He shook his head. 'Not for me, for George. That's why we're talking.'

It came to me then. The photographs on the wall downstairs were of adult women, no nymphets, not even near or pretend nymphets. Paul D'Amico said he disapproved strongly of his brother's policy of using very young girls and had discontinued it in the Coolangatta establishment.

'Lance Harris has supplied young girls for years. A couple, I regret to say, were actually underage and a few others of uncertain age were brought into the country illegally. Christ, bad shit was headed off only by the greatest good luck and some astute payments. I've urged George to change but he won't.'

'Why not?'

He sipped his drink, obviously trying to decide how much to tell me. He shrugged and for the first time looked uncomfortable.

'It's his penchant and it's profitable. There's some sick people out there. You say the girl Harris has in tow is sixteen?'

'Only just,' I said, 'but more importantly, her father is a very wealthy and influential man. If it comes out that George and Harris had a contract to . . .'

'Did they?'

'That's why I'm here. George approached me in Fitzroy Heads and gave me to understand that he was very pissed off that Harris hadn't . . . delivered. My guess is that Harris built up the value of the . . . package and reneged or stalled on the deal. Probably stalled. If I get her back in one piece her father will bring down a shitstorm on your operation—the young girls, the hiring out to yachties, everything.'

'Christ almighty.'

It's not every day you catch an operator like Paul D'Amico on the hop. Despite all his smoothness, I had no illusions about him. He was in the business of selling sex, but that's been going on probably since we were in the trees, certainly since we were in the caves. All his reactions were business, not morally oriented. To a large extent, so were mine. In the cool, executive surroundings, we stared at each other over the single malts.

'What do you want?' he said.

'The girl, intact, and Harris punished.'

'How severely?'

I shrugged.

'Would you be prepared to . . . smooth over certain details for that result?'

'Yes,' I said.

'Then I think I can help you. Where are you staying?'

'Haven't decided. One of the motels on this strip, I suppose.'

'I recommend the Seabreeze. I could ensure you a good rate.'

'Don't bother. When I get settled I'll let you know. For now you can have my mobile number.'

I tore a leaf from my notebook and wrote it down. He watched me as he finished his drink.

'You're a cautious man, Cliff. May I call you Cliff?'

'No. Are you planning to pull the rug out from under your brother?'

'Now, why would you think that?'

'Just a feeling. I've seen these Cain and Abel set-ups before.'

He stood, brushing non-existent fluff from his immaculate suit. 'I'll be in touch if I can help you to . . . defuse Harris.'

'I might as well tell you I've got other lines of enquiry going on. Could be first come, first served.'

'I'll keep that in mind.'

We went down the stairs and the nicely dressed and carefully made-up woman at the desk gave us both a hundred-watt smile. D'Amico ignored her but I smiled back.

I didn't go to the Seabreeze or any other motel. I was sure D'Amico had the contacts to track me to any of the upper level places. I found a caravan park with cabins, well away from the bright lights. It was cheap and rundown. Check-in procedures were rudimentary—the registration of the car and a scrawled signature. I paid the key deposit and three nights' rent in advance in cash and the overweight man in a singlet and shorts didn't even blink.

I phoned Vaughan, told him where I was and what I'd been doing.

'That's a good start,' he said. 'News to me that Classics has gone adult and that the younger brother is getting stroppy. Do you trust him?'

'Not an inch. How've you been getting on?'

'Bit too early for me to find anything very useful. The girls don't get in much before nine and they don't get a break much before eleven. How about we meet up at midnight and compare notes?'

He named a wine bar along the beachfront strip and gave

me directions. The arrangement suited me; it gave me time
to have a swim in the cabin's slightly scungy pool, take a
shower, have a sleep and find somewhere to eat.

The wine bar was called The Cellar but it was at street
level. It was thinly attended when I arrived shortly before
midnight but Vaughan was already there nursing a glass of
red and munching on a breadstick and bits of cabanossi. He
had a small carafe of the red on the table and I poured myself
a glass.

'D'Amico been in touch?' he said.

'Fair go. It's only been a few hours.'

'It's a bit of race, isn't it? To see who comes up with the
goods first.'

'No, mate. I'll pay you for your time and effort whatever
the result, win, lose or draw.'

'Still sounds like a race, but okay. I haven't exactly drawn
a blank but a precise name would've helped. You wouldn't
believe how many strippers have names starting with D,
including one Dee Dee.'

I laughed. 'Is there a Desdemona?'

'What?'

'Doesn't matter. I was told she might be an ex-stripper.
That suggests a certain maturity.'

'Yeah, I used that. You haven't asked how much money
I went through.'

'I don't care. It isn't my money and I'll let you in on something. The client once posted a reward of two hundred and fifty grand for information. I persuaded him to cancel it.'

He stared at me. 'You must be nuts.'

'I wanted a clear field, no treasure hunters.'

'I get it, but you're still nuts.' He took a good pull on his wine and finished off a length of breadstick. The beginnings of a smile spread over his face. I raised my glass to him.

'Okay, let's have it.'

He pulled out a notebook. 'There's a couple of possibilities. First . . .'

The relative quiet of the place was interrupted by the arrival of two men—both big, one in a suit, one in the uniform of the Queensland police force. The uniform adjusted the belt carrying his pistol as they approached our table. The suit stepped in front of him and produced a wallet. He flipped it open to show a warrant card. I had a sense of movement around me as some of the clients edged away.

'Cliff Hardy?'

I recognised him; I'd dealt with him before when I worked with Vaughan on the errant husband case. It hadn't been a happy association.

'Yes,' I said, 'and you're Sergeant . . .?'

'Detective Senior Sergeant Cantini. I want you to accompany us to the Coolangatta police station.'

I opened my hands. 'I'm here having a quiet chat and a

drink with a professional colleague. Why would you want to interrupt us like that?'

He was bulky, stubbled and looked tired. 'Your so-called professional colleague is a nuisance, like you. You're wanted for an interview on the subject of the murder of Paul D'Amico.'

14

I sat in an interview room for about an hour while telephones rang in the police station, people looked curiously at me through the glass panel in the door and no one brought me a cup of coffee. A civilian at the reception desk had asked politely for my ID and I handed it over. He tapped keys on his computer before handing it back. As Cantini escorted me to the interview room, I heard the desk man making a phone call and using my name.

It was past 1.00 am and I was yawning, despite my late-afternoon nap, when a man in shirtsleeves and no tie came into the room carrying two take-away coffees on a cardboard tray. He was in his fifties, at a guess, with grey in his hair and stress in eyes that blinked too rapidly. He put the coffees on the table and sat, almost suppressing a relieved sigh.

'Is this by way of apology?' I said.

'Not exactly,' he said. 'You just happen to be one of the

last people to see D'Amico alive and so you were . . . a person of interest. I'm Detective Inspector Horsfield. I hope Rafa didn't give you too bad a time.'

'Rafa?'

'Senior Sergeant Raffaello Cantini. He gets toey when members of the Italian community come into focus.'

'Hence the belligerence?'

'If you like.'

I sipped the coffee through the slit in the top—black, no sugar. 'What happened?'

'He was badly beaten and then drowned.'

'Where? When?'

He gave a weary groan and did a joint-creaking stretch before drinking some coffee. 'I don't know how to deal with you, Hardy. What do you think this is—your fucking investigation?'

I didn't say anything, sensing that what he'd said had felt uncomfortably close to the truth for him.

'I don't like people in your game turning up and not reporting to us, but I'd like to cooperate with you as far as I can, for now. We won't know until after the autopsy whether he was dead when he went into the water or if the water did the job. He was a mess either way.'

'That's tough. I only met him briefly today. He seemed, let's say, more approachable than his brother.'

'That's it. We need to know everything about your dealings with the D'Amicos.'

'What do you know already?'

'You're determined to play it tight, aren't you? All right, we know you went to his place of business today and had a discussion. The receptionist said you were aggressive.'

'At first, or after the discussion?'

'She didn't say.'

'And then?'

'You seem to have dropped out of sight. That's why Cantini came on a bit strong.'

'How did he get on to me?'

'He picked up some information about Turnbull sniffing around. He knew you'd had dealings with him before and he knew his hangouts.'

'That's pretty good detective work.'

'I'll tell Rafa you said so. It might make him less antagonistic, although I wouldn't bet on it. You're up here working on something. What is it?'

I took my time over the coffee and then shook my head. 'It's not that simple, Inspector. I have a client, an important one, and a colleague.'

'We could make it difficult for you and your colleague to do a bloody thing.'

'Not if you want useful information from me.'

'Have you got useful information?'

I shrugged and looked at my watch. 'Could be. He was alive ten or so hours ago. There's no rush. You need to get an autopsy report and trace D'Amico's movements . . .'

'And yours.'

'Don't bother—I went for a swim and a sleep and a feed. I kept the bill from the café. I need some time to talk to my client and Vaughan Turnbull. Let's say by tomorrow afternoon I might be able to help you.'

I thought he was going to explode but he held himself in. 'I could charge you with obstructing a police investigation.'

'You'd be a fool to do that. I'm willing to cooperate on certain terms. Your choice.'

'You're incredible.'

'Inspector, I've been in business a very long time and I've had my ups and downs with the police. I don't like the way things've shaped up here recently but that's not my problem. I've got a job to do and a client to protect. Our interests might be the same in some ways, probably are, but . . . I hope I've made my point.'

He stood, joints creaking again. 'Tomorrow afternoon you said. Okay, right here, one o'clock sharp!'

'Tomorrow's Sunday.'

'I'm not a churchgoer and I doubt you are either. Be here!'

I nodded. I had to let him have a win.

'Tell the front desk where you're staying and leave your mobile number.'

'I need a ride back to my car.'

'All right, all right. Bugger off.'

*

113

The Sunday morning newspaper carried an account of Paul D'Amico's death. He'd been found floating in the water near a small jetty adjacent to the huge marina. He'd been identified by the documents he carried and by an employee. He was forty-two and was described as a manager of several adult services businesses and as a sportsman.

I rang Vaughan Turnbull, who'd been reading the same newspaper. 'That's a nice description,' he said. 'I suppose he did hit the odd golf ball. Did the cops grill you? That Cantini's a hard case.'

'Not really,' I said. 'We came to an arrangement.'

'With Cantini? You're kidding. He's pretty dirty himself and he sees us as part of the general slime pool.'

'With his boss, Horsfield.'

'Ah, that's different.'

'What d'you know about him?'

'Struggling to stay afloat, if you'll excuse the expression, in the present circumstances, against the hard-liners the previous government pushed forward. He must've gone out on a limb for you.'

It hadn't seemed like that at the time but, if Vaughan's assessment of the power play inside the police force was right, it could look that way and had implications.

'So he'd be looking for a quick result?'

'He needs one. I've got some mates in the lower ranks. The word is he's after a job with the federal police. There's some who don't want him to get it, for obvious reasons.'

'Knows too much and might get brave under the right conditions?'

'Exactly.'

'Jesus, this case was tricky enough without copper politics in the mix. I don't want you to get in trouble with the locals. I know how hard that makes things.'

'Good. I'm no hero.'

'Okay, my line of enquiry ended with D'Amico. You were about to tell me something when Cantini came in. Give it to me now and I'll run with it. I'll see you right money-wise and you can take a holiday.'

'Not on the phone, Cliff. Come to the office.'

I checked out of the caravan park, which had begun to depress me. I was working on a big money case. I wanted a clean pool, air-conditioning, a mini-bar and no cockroaches, and there was no point now in hiding from Paul D'Amico.

The day was warm and sticky. The forecast had promised a breeze but it hadn't arrived yet. I drove to the marina, parked and strolled around. The small, basic, weather-battered jetty near where Paul D'Amico's body was found was more than a hundred metres away from the upmarket part of the marina in a small, seaweed-choked cove. I wondered what the smooth-suited well-groomed man I'd met had been doing there.

I asked a bloke working on his small yacht what the jetty was used for.

He was mahogany-tanned with salt- and sun-bleached hair. His faded blue eyes took pity on a landlubber.

'You can tie up here for a bit. It's like short-term parking when you can't afford the marina.'

'Just you here now?'

'The cops shooed us away after they found the body. I sneaked in this morning, happy to find a spot.'

'You weren't here yesterday then?'

'Nope.'

I wished him happy sailing.

I drove to Vaughan's office address and parked closer this time and in the shade. I climbed the stairs wondering what Vaughan had to tell me that couldn't be said over the phone. Sunday and the building felt empty.

The door to the small outer office was open and I walked in. Vaughan appeared in the doorway to his office.

'I'm sorry, Cliff,' he said.

I felt a savage grip at the top of my neck. I shot both elbows back hard but there was nothing there and in the next instant there was nothing anywhere.

15

I came up out of it gradually and reluctantly. I felt as though I was swimming deep in dark water, unsure which way was up, and not wanting to get it wrong. The place I was in wouldn't stay still; it was tipping and rocking and the darkness was shot through with flashes of light that I slowly realised were visual versions of the pain in my neck.

I surfaced. I was lying propped up on a plastic and metal recliner on the deck of a yacht that was sailing through what felt like calm waters under a light wind. A canopy gave me shade from the bright sun, but when I tried to move I felt the plastic restraints that shackled me to the recliner.

George D'Amico was sitting on a chair a metre away. The sleek suit and smooth grooming were gone; he wore jeans and a T-shirt, deck shoes without socks. Dark bristles sprouted with a touch of grey on his olive-skinned face.

'Hardy,' he said. 'Good to see you back with us. I didn't realise you'd had heart problems. I was worried for a while that you mightn't make it. That carotid grip's a serious thing.'

I concentrated on blinking to rid myself of blurred vision, breathing deeply to slow my pulse and working my tongue around inside my mouth to get some saliva running. I didn't say anything. D'Amico watched me and nodded.

'Recovery techniques. Very impressive, but then, you've been through some tough spots in your time, haven't you? We noticed a couple of healed bullet wounds as well as the zipper scar; not to mention the busted nose.'

You can only maintain the initiative with silence for so long and the time had run out.

'Nothing recent,' I said.

He shifted a little and gazed out at the water, visible to him but not to me. 'But how would you go weighed down and dumped five kilometres out to sea?'

I turned my head very carefully to look around. I knew nothing about boat maintenance, but everything I could see that I guessed should be scrubbed, polished and tied down was.

'I don't see an Early Cooker or a tub of cement.'

D'Amico smiled. 'You're a piece of work, Hardy.'

Another American expression, I thought. *The boys have either been there or they watch a lot of television.*

'Maybe,' I said. 'But I didn't kill your brother, if that's what you're thinking.'

'No? And what's *your* thinking on the matter?'

'I don't think that well under restraint. With an aching head and a dry throat.'

D'Amico raised his voice. 'Serge! The tin snips.'

I heard footsteps and felt someone bending over me. Tin snips will take a finger. I closed my eyes. D'Amico laughed; I heard the blades clip closed and my left wrist was free.

'Get the man a couple of Panadols and a drink,' D'Amico said. 'Make it a Crownie. Sorry, we haven't got any Little Creatures.'

I opened my eyes and drew in a deep breath of the salty air. 'You've done this intimidation stunt before.'

'Right. The last guy pissed his pants, but they got a good wash after.'

I flexed my hand and wrist. 'You're talking too much and too fancy. You're worried, George.'

The soft footsteps returned and two capsules dropped into my lap. A Crown Lager stubby was placed gently beside me on the recliner. I took a look at the pills and smelled and licked them. Then I swallowed them down dry.

'Tough guy,' D'Amico said.

I lifted the bottle and took a small sip, letting it wash over the tastebuds. Then I tilted it up and drank half in a series of long gulps. I put the bottle down within easy reach.

'To return to the original question,' he said. 'Who do you think killed Paul?'

'Not interested in why?'

'Learn who, and why'd become obvious.'

'Not necessarily, but anyway I had two people in mind—you and Lance Harris.'

'I wouldn't kill my own brother.'

'Been known to happen.'

'Bullshit. The way I see it, you're responsible. You got him looking for Harris.'

'Did I?'

'The room you were in at Classics is bugged. I heard the recording. If Harris killed him, you're to blame in a way. I can find Harris, so you're sort of surplus to requirements. Everything you have with you was in your car. It wouldn't be too hard to make you disappear.'

He was serious now. I was sure he was worried—threatening, but not as sure of himself as he pretended, but I didn't know why. Had things with Paul got really out of hand? Had he sent someone to talk to him and it had gone wrong? It was a possibility. How deeply was he involved with Harris and did he have anything to fear from my finding him first? I had no answers and all the questions could easily add up to his point that there was no need for me. I tried hard to think of something that would convince him otherwise.

I said, 'Are you sure you can find Harris? I've been chasing him all over the fucking Pacific and up the coast. He's slippery.'

I drank the rest of the beer. I could smash the bottle on the deck and cut the other restraint, but then what? D'Amico was younger and fitter than me and Serge obviously wasn't the only crew member. Almost as if he'd read my mind, D'Amico stretched his leg and kicked the bottle across the deck.

'I hear the cops pulled you in?'

I nodded.

'What did you tell them?'

I briefly considered mentioning my wealthy client as a counterweight but decided against it. If he'd heard my discussion with his brother he'd know about him and apparently wasn't concerned.

'Not much,' I said. 'They're expecting me to show up. . .' I squinted down at my watch, '. . . in about a quarter of an hour.'

D'Amico gave a bored shrug. 'You're not going to make it.'

Off to one side there was the roar of an engine and a booming voice sounded above the slap of the waves and the sails.

'Ahoy, *Classic Belle*. You are to change course. You will be escorted back to the police dock at Coolangatta. Acknowledge!'

Serge was instantly on deck. 'Boss?'

D'Amico's boredom changed to something like extreme anger. 'You fucker.'

'Nothing to do with me. I'm as surprised as you are. Relieved though.'

'Boss?'

'Let me think. Anything hot on board?'

'A Glock and some pills, I think.'

'Make sure and ditch them. Then do as they say.'

I jiggled my shackled wrist so that the recliner bounced a little. 'Hey, Serge,' I shouted. 'How about those tin snips and another Crownie?'

16

It took three hours and some very unhappy and angry cops to resolve things. By the time the *Classic Belle* tied up at the police dock I was sitting in a chair on the deck chatting amiably to D'Amico. He'd given me back my wallet and keys. We were hauled off to the police station, where Horsfield informed me that a member of the public had seen me being taken forcibly on board the yacht and had contacted the police.

'That's an exaggeration,' I said.

'You went willingly?'

'You could say I was encouraged to go.'

'When I heard about it I sent the boat. It looked like an attempt to prevent you talking to me today.'

'It wasn't. D'Amico didn't know anything about that.'

'What did he want?'

'His brother's murderer.'

Horsfield snorted his mock amusement. 'Did you suggest he look in a mirror?'

'To tell you the truth, I did say something along those lines.'

'And now you're protecting him.'

'There was no harm done.'

'Why are you wincing every time you move your head?'

'A touch of sciatica.'

'You could lay an assault charge. I could arrest him.'

'He'd be out within hours and you know it.'

Horsfield gave one of his tired smiles. 'It might interest you to know that some of the changes up here you don't approve of give us a bit more leeway than you have down in Sydney.'

'Maybe so, but what would be the point? If he killed his brother it'd be best to let him move about while you look for evidence. If he didn't, given his motivation and resources, he might actually find out who did.'

'Oh, right. And this ties in with your important case you were going to consult your client about and then talk to me. The way I see it you've got someone else in mind as the killer—your target, let's say.'

'You're warm.'

'You bet I'm warm, I'm fucking hot.'

What Vaughan had told me about Horsfield was showing now. He was as honest as a Queensland cop could be and he desperately wanted a result. That knowledge gave me room to manoeuvre.

'I haven't talked to my client yet and I need to talk to Vaughan Turnbull before I can be more helpful to you.'

'Well you're out of luck there. Turnbull's disappeared.'

'What d'you mean?'

'What I say. Not sighted or contactable since last night. Why don't you ask your friend D'Amico about it?'

I had nothing to say, feeling well out-played at that point. Horsfield stood and, against my usual practice in these situations, I let him take the dominant position.

'You can go,' he said. 'Your car's parked down at the marina. I hope it's got a ticket and you can fucking well get there under your own steam.'

'Last thing,' I said. 'The call you responded to. Was it anonymous?'

'Yes, but convincing. Pommy accent. He knew your name and described you in detail. "Big, dark, knockabout bastard", I think he said. Do you know who it was?'

'No idea,' I said, but I was lying.

There was no sign of D'Amico when I left the police station. I caught a taxi back to the marina and wandered around until I found the car. No ticket. The fact that D'Amico had taken charge of my car chilled me a little—it put weight behind his threat. If he'd decided to dump me at sea the next step would have been to disappear the car and there are many ways to do that.

There was no shade. The car's interior was like a sauna under the late afternoon sun, with all the surfaces hot to the touch. I felt wrung out and frustrated. It seemed as though things were slipping out of my hands; an uncomfortable feeling. I grabbed the phone from the glove box and retreated to a small nearby park where I could sit under a tree and hope for a breeze.

There were a couple of texts and messages unrelated to the Fonteyn case that felt as if they belonged to another life and I ignored them. But one message was of the here and now: *Hardy, Colin Cameron. I've saved your arse I believe and we have things to talk about. I'm sure you'll have talked your way out of any trouble. I'm staying at the Surfside hotel and I'm planning for it to be on your bill, so you better get over here toot sweet.*

I rang his number but was told to leave a message. Cameron was on a roll.

The Surfside was a five-star hotel and Cameron had installed himself in style in a room close to the rooftop pool, well away from the traffic noise. I marched past him when he opened the door with a drink in his hand. I had an overnight bag in my hand and a towel over my shoulder.

'I'm going to have a shower and change my clothes,' I said. 'Be nice if you had a drink ready for me when I come out.'

I barely gave him a glance, just enough to see his jaw drop. He spluttered over his drink but I was in the bathroom before he could say anything. I took my time. After the crappy cabin, the carotid pinch and sweating it out with D'Amico and the police, the cool, beautifully appointed bathroom was welcome. I hadn't realised how much strain I'd been under until I saw my face in the mirror. There were dark smudges under my eyes and the grooves on my dial were almost as deep as Mick Jagger's.

The room was virtually a suite, with a second small room containing a single bed off to one side. I tossed my bag onto the bed.

'What're you doing?' Cameron said.

'If I'm paying, we're sharing. Where's that drink?'

He'd had too much sun of late. His face and ears were pink. He had the kind of skin that requires a hat whenever the sun is out.

'I saved your life,' he said.

I brushed past him on the way to the mini-bar. 'How do you figure that?'

'You were being taken out to be deep-sixed.'

'Possibly. The issue was still in doubt when the cops arrived.'

Cameron was sitting in an armchair, one of two facing a long, low couch with a coffee table in between. I opened the mini-bar and nodded my approval of the contents.

'What're you having?' I said.

'Gin and tonic.'

'Good choice. Any lemon?'

'Lime juice.'

'That'll do.'

I made myself a light drink and stretched out on the couch. 'Okay, Col. Tell me all about your adventures.'

I patronised him and was thoroughly unpleasant as I interrupted his narrative, throwing in sceptical asides. I was trying to keep him off-balance and get him under control but without much success. As he talked he gained in confidence and it became clear that he had an ace in the hole that he was protecting.

Cameron had followed me to Ballina and Fitzroy Heads and picked up my trail to Coolangatta. I'd underestimated his investigative skills. He'd fallen in with some dope smokers who knew Harris, had bought from him, and knew he was targeting the Coolangatta kids. When he got there he looked for somewhere cheap to stay and by sheer luck saw me leaving the caravan park on my way to meet Vaughan and followed me in his rental car. I waited for him to chortle about that but he didn't.

'I saw them carry you out,' he said. 'They were trying to make it look as if they were supporting a drunk. I saw one of them take your car to the marina and I saw them put you on the yacht. Then I called the police and you haven't thanked me.'

'You didn't need to butt in.'

'Against that lot? Come on. But I got a fair bit of it on film in case they killed you.'

The gin on top of my tiredness had mellowed me and I had to laugh. I waved my hand at the comfortable and expensive surroundings.

'You're all right, Col. Thanks. It was a very tight spot. But I have to say I'm surprised at your attitude and all this.'

That was the first time I'd let up on him and he showed his appreciation by fixing new drinks for us both.

'That's okay, Cliff. I think we're a team again and as such we need to renegotiate our arrangement.'

'Yes?'

'Yes. I need to tap into some more of the Fonteyn funds.'

'It'd take more than what you've done for me to swing that, grateful as I am. Are you telling me you know where Harris and the girl are? Maybe you've got footage.'

'I wish. No, not that much, but I've got Vaughan Turnbull and I know what he wanted to tell you before George D'Amico shanghaied you.'

17

'What do you mean you've *got* him?'

'I mean I know where he is and I've convinced him that it's in his best interests to throw in with me and make a serious dollar out of this business rather than just accept handouts from you.'

'I thought you were only concerned about rebuilding your career.'

'I've revised my agenda, and don't blame Turnbull too much. D'Amico really put the frighteners on him and he's looking to relocate or take a long holiday. Either way, that takes money.'

He was cocky and he had reason to be. What he'd said had reawakened a worry I'd had. How did D'Amico know to locate me through Vaughan? The obvious answer was that he had a police contact. If that was true, there was plenty of reason for Vaughan to think about relocating.

'Things might work out your way,' I said. 'It'll depend on how good this information of Vaughan's is. You've been in this thing almost since the beginning. How would you evaluate it, putting your own interests aside?'

'Fair question.' Cameron finished his drink and crunched the ice cubes, looking thoughtful.

'I'd say, judging from his attitude and expectations, that it's very good. Not decisive but definitely something to follow up.'

'Okay, I'll talk to Fonteyn. You can clear out while I do it.'

'Of course. I hope your Amex is in the black. I've been running up some serious expenses here. I tried my card but it's tapped out.'

He got up, collected sunglasses, wallet and the door card.

'Leave the card. Get another one for yourself at the desk.'

It was petty sparring but sometimes you need that before you get down to the serious business. I dug in my bag for the heart-monitoring medications I'd neglected to take. I swallowed a couple of the pills down and dialled Gerard Fonteyn's private number. He recognised the caller.

'Mr Hardy, I've been hoping to hear from you. What progress?'

It's always an awkward situation approaching a client for more money without having anything solid to report. It was a bit different this time in that I already had access to the money, the substantial residue of the twenty grand I'd been authorised to draw on at the beginning, but I felt a responsibility to clear further solid expenditure with Fonteyn. I gave him an outline of what had happened without the dramatics and said there was a way forward but that it'd be costly and I wasn't sure how costly.

'Don't tell me you need to buy a yacht.'

I laughed, breaking the tension I was feeling. My respect for him went up.

'No, but the man who approached you initially says he has important information and he's driving a hard bargain and . . .'

'Do you believe she's still alive?'

I knew something was going on that I didn't understand. Harris hadn't sold Juliana to George D'Amico. Why not? Was she the girl of his dreams?

'I do, yes.'

'Then spend whatever you need. I'll have someone contact your bank and arrange a line of credit for you. Would a hundred thousand be enough?'

I assured him it would. He asked if he could be of help in any other way. Was there anyone he could call? It was a sensible suggestion and I told him I'd let him know. I realised I hadn't touched the drink while I'd been speaking and that I was sweating.

I called Cameron's mobile.

'Get the green light?' he said.

'For you, it's a yellow light. Where are you?'

'In the bar. Where d'you think?'

'I'll be there in a few minutes.'

'Good. You'll be meeting an old friend—you're paying for him as well.'

The bar was cool and quiet with muted lighting and music. Cameron and Vaughan Turnbull were at a table with their drinks and bowls of nuts. Both had mobile phones in their hands and Cameron appeared to be demonstrating the functions of his. A new toy, I assumed. He was going the whole hog.

Turnbull looked sheepish as I approached and almost got to his feet deferentially, just restraining himself.

'I'm sorry, Cliff,' he said.

I sat. 'Are you? For what?'

He pointed to his neck where two pale overlapping bandaids stood out against his tanned skin. 'D'Amico's offsider had a gun. He jammed it into my neck.'

I nodded. 'Serge. A Glock. It's at the bottom of the sea now, thanks to Colin here.'

Turnbull picked up his drink, rum and Coke at a guess. 'It got too heavy for me. I'm glad you . . .'

'Forget it,' I said. 'I'm more interested in what arrangements you've come to with your pal Col.'

Turnbull was on his feet now in a very different frame of mind. 'Fuck you, Hardy! I'm out of business here. D'Amico swings a lot of weight and . . .'

I made a placatory gesture with both hands. 'Easy, easy. And he has police connections. I don't blame you, Vaughan.'

Turnbull sat down. 'Yes you do, but fuck you anyway.'

'With all that resolved,' Cameron said, 'are we ready to talk terms?'

'What do you want?' I said. Before either could answer, I went on. 'I'll hear what Vaughan has to say. If I like it I'll arrange for ten thousand to be paid into his bank account. He can have one more night here at my expense. Drink all the booze he wants and watch as much porn as he cares to. Then he strolls away.'

'You're a bastard, Hardy,' Turnbull said.

'I know, but your story stinks.' I reached across the table quickly and peeled the bandaids away. There was no wound. 'You told D'Amico I was coming to you. I don't know how, maybe through Cantini. Doesn't matter. The offer still holds as long as I'm a hundred per cent sure you haven't told D'Amico what it is you have to sell.'

'I haven't.'

'I think I believe you. You're smart enough to know that I'd pay for it at the going rate, even before Col came on the scene and upped the ante. D'Amico'd just take it and tell you to keep quiet or do something rather worse.'

'Okay, okay,' Cameron said. 'Now, what about me?'

'You're a separate case,' I said. I took out my voice recorder and put it on the table. 'Let's hear what Vaughan has to say and while we're at it, let's have a drink. Mine's a Fourex Light.'

C'mon, Col, do the honours and see if you can rustle me up a sandwich. I haven't had anything to eat today at all and I need something to blot up the grog.'

'A Fourex Light isn't grog,' Turnbull said.

'It is on top of two Crownies on D'Amico's boat courtesy of you and a G 'n' T with Col.'

Cameron gave me a sour look as he left the table. He made to pick up his mobile but I put my hand over it, determined to keep him on a tight leash.

Turnbull cleared his throat. 'I found Harris's wife. Her professional name's Desiree. Everyone just pronounces it Desire. She's semi-retired, if you take my meaning.'

'I think so. What's her real name?'

'Who knows? Anyway, Harris and the girl paid her a visit. She lives on a boat moored in one of the canals.'

'Boats, boats, I'm sick of fucking boats.'

'Well you're going to hear a bit more about them.'

'Go on.'

'According to Desiree, they used her place for a night or two to sell some drugs. They needed money to get to Sydney.'

'Why Sydney?'

'That's the screwiest part of it. Harris wants to marry the girl. He's obsessed with her. But she won't tell him anything about herself, not her name, her age, nothing. Harris says he knows people in Sydney who can get her papers—birth certificate, a passport, Medicare fucking card. Then they'll take off for Hong Kong or somewhere.'

'You got this for how much?'

'Five hundred, half of what you gave me, and a lot of pricey booze. She's a far-gone alky and . . .'

'Hold on, I need to think.' I switched off the recorder and Turnbull sat back looking apprehensive. Cameron returned with the drinks and a bulging salad sandwich. While I was wolfing it down Cameron and Turnbull exchanged looks. Turnbull shook his head and shrugged when Cameron asked what was going on.

'He's thinking,' Turnbull said.

'What about?'

I washed down the last of the sandwich with a swig of the beer. I switched the recorder on.

'Okay, Vaughan,' I said. 'That's all very interesting but it doesn't lead anywhere and it's not worth ten grand. Sydney's a big place and Harris can't finance false papers and a trip to Hong Kong on the sale of some grass and a few pills. There has to be more that you've told Cameron. Now tell me and earn your money.'

Cameron relaxed in his chair. 'So that's where we're at. Tell him, Turnbull.'

'Harris told Desiree he'd killed Paul D'Amico. Said it was an accident, in a fight over the girl. Sort of.'

'Hard to believe. What's the girl doing while this is going on?'

'Stoned but amused. Desiree says she seemed to find it funny that Harris wanted to marry her. Desiree knows men and women inside and out, back to front, if you know what I mean. She reckons the girl can get Harris to do whatever she wants.'

'I still can't see where this gets me.'

Turnbull nodded. 'Harris's putting his yacht up for sale.'

I shrugged. 'So?'

'This is the clincher, Cliff,' Cameron said. 'This is what Turnbull wouldn't tell me—the name of the broker here in Coolangatta who must have the papers with Harris's signature and must know how to contact him in Sydney. Vaughan here says he'll only tell you when he's sure of the money.'

Turnbull said, 'I would've told you this, Cliff, when we got together in the wine bar and you were going to put me . . . on wages, shall we say. Before I knew how big this really was and how fucking heavy it could get. Cantini's interruption has cost your client a lot of money.'

'Don't fret about it, Vaughan,' Cameron said. Slightly pissed, he did a fair Paul McCartney impression: '*The long and winding road . . .*'

18

Vaughan Turnbull had a sense of the dramatic. He took a notebook from his pocket, tore out a page and wrote on it. Pushed it towards me.

'That's his name and my bank details.'

I pushed it back.

'And where to find Desiree.'

'Why?'

I shrugged. 'I might learn a bit more and Colin here might want to take a photo.'

'She'd need an hour to prepare.'

'Just do it, Vaughan,' I said. I took out my phone. 'I'll get busy with your transfer, but don't press your luck. Don't contact Cantini or George D'Amico.'

He scribbled some more and I took the note.

'Why would I do that?'

'Mate, I don't even know why you've done what you've

already done, not really. I'm just saying—give me a clear run at this. And these details better be right or I'll come looking for you.'

Turnbull didn't touch the fresh drink Cameron had brought him, a scotch and ice. He pushed back his chair and walked away. Cameron sloshed it into his own glass.

'You're hard on him,' he said.

'I'm hard on anyone who buggers me around. Keep that in mind.'

He worked on his now double scotch while I got my bank online and transferred nine thousand, nine hundred and ninety-nine dollars to Turnbull's account. When I looked up Cameron was smiling at me expectantly.

'Time to talk terms with me, Cliff.'

I shook my head. 'Not yet it isn't. You've booked yourself in for the long ride. You're going with me to talk to Desiree and then to pay a call to . . .' I looked at the note . . . 'Bruce McBain of Marine Services Pty Ltd. Bring your camera.'

Cameron was doing himself proud; he'd hired a flash SUV in Ballina, which he said had completely drained his credit card. I was resolved to get as much work out of him as possible so I said we'd take his car.

'I'm going to need funds,' he said.

'You're going to earn them. Let's get a map and find out where this canal is.'

We bought a map at a petrol station and located the canal. It turned out to be more of a creek, or it had been before the developments got going. It was flanked by big houses and apartment blocks that would be flooded if the global warming predictions came true. The buildings were over-elaborate showpieces, no loss if the waters rose. A houseboat was moored near where the original creek had undergone its makeover. There was a postage-stamp-sized jetty at the end of a track that led from the road down through a patch of scrubby land. Mangroves pressed against the mooring and the spot looked as though it'd be swampy when it rained.

We got out of the car and Cameron slapped at a mosquito. 'Ross River fever country,' he said.

'Let's keep it cheerful, shall we?'

'What're you hoping to get from her?'

'More.'

We walked down to the jetty. It had seen better days, like the houseboat itself. It was shabby with peeling paint and rusty metal fittings. The sun was getting low in a cloudy sky and the mangroves cut down on the light. It was a gloomy scene.

'Heart of darkness,' Cameron said.

'Cut it out,' I said, but he was right. I moved gingerly onto the jetty. The planks sagged a little but held. Two steps took me to where a section of the boat rail was hinged to form a gate. I undid the catch and stepped onto the deck of the boat. It didn't move at all. The water in the creek was low and the boat had settled on the bottom.

Cameron was right behind me. 'At least we won't get seasick,' he said.

His chatter was annoying but I knew it was down to nervousness so I didn't say anything. Later, maybe.

'Anybody home?' I called.

That startled a seagull into taking off from the rail but brought no other response. I called again, with the same result. I'd been on houseboats on the Hawkesbury in jaunty times and knew where the living quarters were likely to be. We moved forward, past the wheelhouse cabin and along to where steps led down below the deck.

Mangrove mud is smelly and the deck of the houseboat hadn't been swabbed in a long time. Cigarette butts had been stamped into it and unnamed liquids spilled, but the smell coming up from below was something different and there was a humming sound that wasn't mosquitoes.

I gestured for Cameron not to touch anything and to stay back while I went down the steps. The space at the bottom is usually called the saloon. Typically, it contains a long, bolted-down table with bench seats on either side. Social area. Same here, but a woman was lying along one of the seats with her legs splayed out and her arms drooping. Flies buzzed around the slash that had cut her throat through to the vertebrae.

I swore.

'What?' Cameron said. I was blocking his view on the narrow steps.

'Have you ever seen violent death close up?'

'Quite a few times.'

'Kept your dinner down?'

'After the first one, sure.'

I backed up. 'Come down and get the best shot you can. Don't touch anything at all or drop anything. Make it quick and then we're off.'

He edged past me and I heard the sharp intake of his breath. I went back on deck and breathed the sultry, unclean air. Cameron came back and tapped his camera.

'Got it. Very nasty, but not the worst I've . . .'

'Let's go.'

We retreated to the boarding point and I used the sleeve of my shirt to wipe down where I'd touched the rail and the gate. We went quickly back to the car. The area could be seen from high levels of some of the buildings but I didn't notice any movement. I told Cameron to start the engine and move off quietly. When we'd made several turns I relaxed. To give him his due, Cameron was calm and silent, concentrating on his driving. He said, 'Who the hell did that?'

'Who knows? Harris in a rage? An unhappy client?'

'The girl, off her face?'

'Don't even think it.'

Eventually, with the CBD in sight, I told him to pull over and asked to see the photograph.

There was no doubt that the man had the talent; he'd caught the full horror of the scene with the light falling on the wound, the distributed blood and, with Desiree's head turned slightly to one side, a single staring eye.

'That should do it,' I said.

'Do what?'

'We're going to see this marine broker, Bruce McBain. I'm betting he and Harris go back a long way and that he knew Desiree. If that picture doesn't jolt the information we want out of him, nothing will.'

'What if . . .?'

'Yeah, what if she told whoever killed her about the sale of the yacht? No way to be absolutely sure but if he's been approached by anyone involved in this mess, we'll know when we see him.'

'If he's alive.'

'That's a point.'

McBain's office was a stone's throw from the marina in a long, low, stylish building with tinted windows, several flagpoles flying various flags unknown to me and underground parking for the occupants. Visitors could please themselves.

'Pricey place,' Cameron said.

'Don't be too impressed. Everyone in it's probably in hock to someone else.'

'You're a cynic's cynic, Hardy.'

We went into the building and located Marine Services on the first floor. We took the stairs and went down a corridor towards the back. Last office on the right. I pushed at the door and stood aside to let a young woman who'd been on the point of opening it step through.

'We're closed,' she said.

'Not quite.' I flipped my wallet quickly open and shut, showing the licence. 'Police. Mr McBain in? Good. I think you can go, Ms . . .'

'McBain. I'm his daughter.'

I smiled reassuringly. 'Then we'll know how to reach you if we need to. Thank you. Step aside, Constable.'

Cameron moved; she edged past him and hurried away.

'IPO. That's an offence,' Cameron said.

'One of many.'

I went past Ms McBain's desk with all its appurtenances neatly arranged and opened the door behind it. A fat man in shirtsleeves was standing looking out at the marina. Too fat to spin, he turned slowly.

'What the hell . . .'

'Take it easy, Mr McBain. We need a few minutes of your time.'

'You have to make an appointment.'

'This can't wait. Please sit down.'

I was watching him closely. He showed no signs of anything frightening happening to him lately, just extreme annoyance at being accosted when he was ready to sign off. Tall but very overweight, tanned but with too high a colour under the tan, he looked us over and decided he might as well sit down. Just doing that—two steps and a careful lowering—was an effort that had him sucking in a much-needed breath.

'You're brokering the sale of Lance Harris's boat.'

'Yacht. Yes.'

'Pimp boat,' I said. 'It was arranged by . . .' I nodded at Cameron. 'Show him.'

Cameron, who must've watched a few cop shows on TV, was leaning against the wall. He unshipped his camera, fiddled with the controls and put the small image a few centimetres in front of McBain's face.

'Jesus Christ!'

'Not there at the time,' I said. 'Nor were we. Put your head between your legs and pull the wastepaper bin closer if you need to.'

McBain scrabbled in a desk drawer for a packet of pills and clawed two out of the foil. The mug on his desk must have held some dregs of tea or coffee and he used them to swallow the pills. Cameron gave him one more look at the photo and then moved away.

McBain crossed his arms over his chest and coughed. 'I'm a sick man,' he said. 'Who are you?'

'It doesn't matter,' I said. 'You never saw us and you'll never see us again, but if you don't want to meet up with whoever did that to Desiree you'll answer one question and take some advice.'

McBain surprised me by recovering some of the sort of dignity that, oddly, fat men can muster. He still had his blue yacht-club tie tight around his fleshy neck and he loosened it. He took a tissue from the box on his desk and dabbed at his high, moist forehead.

'And what would those things be?'

'First, tell me how you were to contact Harris in Sydney and after that, forget him—and you'd be wise to take a long and far-distant holiday.'

part three

19

On the Qantas flight from Coolangatta to Sydney that evening Cameron sulked. I'd made him leave the room while McBain gave me the information I wanted and I didn't share it with him. He wanted to stay another night at the Surfside but I checked him and Turnbull, who'd already left, out and covered all their charges. I paid what he owed at the airport when he returned the SUV and I dropped off the Mitsubishi but he still wasn't happy.

'You could've at least booked us business class.'

'Mate. Give it a rest.'

'Don't forget I saved your life.'

'Maybe you did and you've been useful since, but I'm not your gravy train. I'll give you some more money and you can stay in Sydney until this gets settled. I might need to call on you again. Nothing to stop you getting work and earning a quid yourself.'

'I'm on a visitor's visa.'

'You wouldn't be the first to fiddle that.'

'I could approach Fonteyn personally. Tell him what I know.'

'What *do* you know?'

'That his daughter's hooked on drugs. That she's manipulating a man who killed another man and that she's possibly an accomplice . . .'

He stopped.

I nodded. 'You see where that's heading. If we're going to come out of this the way we want to, certain things have to be more fully understood and, let's say . . . arranged.'

There was barely time for a drink and a snack on the flight but we had both. Cameron chewed on the twist of lemon from his gin and tonic. 'I see what you mean. A clean outcome could be tricky to organise.'

'Exactly. It's difficult when you're not quite sure who to blame, who to punish and who to protect.'

'Quite the philosopher, aren't you?'

'No, I'm just going along hoping for the best.'

'Who for?'

'For everyone who deserves it.'

'Does that include me?'

'So far.'

Cameron collected the luggage he'd left when he'd arrived in Sydney before scooting off to Ballina. He told me he had friends in the city and would be able to lob in with one or another of them, especially if he was able to pay his way.

I told him to keep his phone charged and tell me where he was day by day.

Before we separated at the airport I got his bank account details and agreed to pay him the balance of the original ten thousand.

'One way and another you've dipped pretty deep into Fonteyn's pocket already,' I said. 'What you're getting now should keep you afloat here for a while.'

'How long will it take you to find them, do you think? It's your city and you've got the contact info.'

'You mean how long will it take to detach a drug-addicted teenager from a homicidal paedophile drug dealer without causing too much collateral damage?'

'Okay, okay, I take the point. But the whole deal has to be part of the outcome. Don't forget, I still have the photographs of the girl and Desiree, and in case you didn't notice I sent them to the Cloud.'

'I'm not forgetting. The girl? That could be worth something to you whether things go right or wrong. Desiree? I wouldn't be sure that having taken that picture is to your advantage.' Then I did a fair but exaggerated impression of his mockney accent. 'Know wot I mean?'

I left him with his cameras and other baggage and caught a cab to Glebe.

*

I emptied my bag. Dumped some clothes in the washing machine and checked the accumulated mail—there was nothing that couldn't wait. Ditto for phone messages. They mostly came to my mobile these days and there was nothing of importance there either.

I rang Megan to tell her I was back.

'You sound tired,' she said.

'Been busy. How're you lot?'

'Okay. We're thinking of buying a house and want your advice.'

'What do I know? I've only ever had one.'

'You *are* tired. Did you get the boys something from Norfolk?'

'How about a machete?'

'What?'

'Never mind. Yes, I got a telescope and a compass from the *Bounty*. Seems they had plastic in those days.'

'How's the investigation?'

'Moving forward, as they say.'

'Weasel words, I'm ashamed of you using language like that. Get some sleep, Cliff.'

I thought about going to the office but decided against it. Didn't like to admit it, but I was mentally as well as physically tired. And I had some serious thinking to do.

Recently, someone had told me that, if I wasn't going to grind my own coffee beans, then keeping the ready-ground stuff in the fridge was the go. Since I'd been doing that my coffee-making had improved and I'd started to buy more upmarket stuff. I brewed up a pot and excavated and microwaved lamb curry with rice. I ate the curry with a glass of red and sat down with a mug of coffee, laced with scotch, to think.

There were several possibilities. One was, in effect, to toss in the towel. If Fonteyn were to blanket the Sydney media about his missing daughter the smell of money could flush Harris out. Against that, Harris could face prosecution for abducting and abusing a minor, not to mention his likely involvement in the death of Paul D'Amico. Then there was his apparent obsession with the girl. That could result in almost any disaster.

McBain had given me a name, a phone number and an address but there were problems with that as well. The name was Philip Harris and McBain didn't know whether it was Lance Harris's brother, father, son, cousin or a simple coincidence of a not uncommon surname. If it was family, how deep did loyalties run? Lance's reputation for letting people down could have an effect. The *Zaca 3* was worth a lot. Blood is thicker than water but not always thicker than money.

And there was the story of Harris wanting papers for his child-bride-to-be. There are ways of going about that and I knew people who could point me in the right direction. That could be a crab-like approach to the matter.

That was as far as my thinking took me. I cleaned up, put the washed clothes in the dryer and arranged the *Bounty*'s telescope and compass on a shelf.

Boats, I thought, *bloody boats*. I climbed the stairs and went to bed.

In the morning Cameron rang to let me know his address in Petersham.

'Give me a ring when you fancy a Portuguese meal.'

'I might do that.'

'Have you decided what to do?'

'Yes,' I said and hung up.

I'd decided on a full frontal approach. Philip Harris lived in Greenwich. I rang the number and got a message telling me to call a mobile number. When I did I got a businesslike voice.

'Philip Harris.'

'Mr Harris, my name's Hardy. I'm a private detective. I'm ringing about Lance Harris. Am I right in thinking he's your . . .?'

'Brother. Yes. What's he done now?'

'I'm keen to contact him about several matters. Could we meet?'

'No. I don't want anything to do with him or with anyone connected with him.'

'He gave your name as a contact to a broker who's selling his yacht and I . . .'

The laugh that came over the line was full-throated and genuine. 'You must be joking. Lance wouldn't sell his boat in a fit unless it was some shonky scheme that he'd come out of with the money *and* the boat. And he wouldn't involve me in anything like that. If I knew where the bastard was I'd set the police on him immediately and hope to recover one tenth of what he's defrauded me of. You've been misinformed. Goodbye.'

I put the phone down and sat back feeling foolish. McBain had been scared out of his wits and I was sure he'd told me what Harris had told him. Leaving a false trail is a standard con man's trick. Did Harris know he was being pursued other than for his involvement with the D'Amicos? It seemed unlikely. Had he told Desiree the truth about his plans for the girl and the future? It seemed to fit his profile.

I went into my office, tidied up some loose ends and checked with my bank. Fonteyn's money was there washing around, ready to be drawn on. I shifted the amount I'd agreed on to Cameron's account and considered my options. Fonteyn's faith in me was almost crippling. I badly wanted to present him with a result he could live with.

People need new identities for all sorts of reasons. Ex-prisoners need a clean sheet, so do sex offenders and bankrupts and those who've over-stayed their visas and don't want to go home. Banned drivers need new licences, failed apprentices need tickets and CEOs need to open accessible offshore accounts.

I'd been very impressed by the last scene in the movie *Killing Them Softly*. Brad Pitt, a hitman, comes into a bar to meet his paymaster after completing some assignments. The paymaster attempts to short-change him. In the background Barack Obama is delivering a campaign speech. It's 2008 and Obama's message has been heard in snippets throughout the film. Now he's talking about the American community. Pitt, cool and menacing, says to the paymaster, 'America's not a community. It's a business. Fuckin' pay me!'

Australia's going the same way. Politics is a business, welfare is a business, health is a business, law has always been a business and identity is big business. The trouble was there are specialists in the identity business and it'd take some deep digging to find who Harris would approach. If he had very good contacts I might not have the time to do it. I was about to make the first of a series of calls when the phone rang.

The voice was familiar but only just. 'Mr Hardy? This is Foster Fonteyn. I have to see you.'

'Why?'

'It . . . it's about Juliana.'

I met Foxy in the Double Bay wine bar where we'd met before. It was late in the morning and the red wine he had in front of him wasn't his first. He looked much older than when I'd first met him. In a way he'd cleaned up his act. He had a neat beard and his clothes showed some sign of having been chosen with care but then neglected. He seemed like someone who'd brushed himself up to apply for a job and hadn't got it. His fingers, twisting the glass, were heavily nicotine-stained and his eyes were bloodshot. He attempted an ingratiating smile that fell well short of the mark.

'I'm in big trouble, Mr Hardy.'

'You've been heading that way for a while, Foxy.'

He flared up. 'You don't know what it's like to be the son of Dr fucking Perfect. You're expected to hit all the runs, kick all the goals, scoop the prize pool. I couldn't do it and I . . . came unstuck.'

'I'm not here to judge you. I'm here to talk about Juliana.'

He gave a bitter laugh and half rose in his chair. 'I'm getting another drink.'

I reached out to his bony shoulder and pushed him down. 'You'll sit there and drink coffee. I don't want you pissed.'

He blinked back tears and sat down. I went to the counter and ordered two long blacks. The place was almost empty and the coffees arrived quickly. I shovelled several spoonsful of raw sugar into his cup and gestured for him to drink. Like a lot of places, this one served its coffee less than piping hot and Foxy was able to swallow a couple of big gulps.

'I'm sending this back to get a hot one. Pull yourself together. You can tell me your troubles, but get to Juliana pretty bloody quick.'

When I got back with the coffee he'd finished his and was shaking pills from a bottle. I stopped him.

'No pills. You're doing this cold turkey.'

'I can't.'

'You'd better. You must've been desperate to call me. Shape up or I'm out of here and you're all on your own.'

He started talking. He said Juliana found life as stultifying as he did but, being better behaved and able to live up to the expectations, which were fewer in her case, she suffered in silence.

'What sort of expectations? He doesn't seem an overly ambitious parent to me.'

'Yeah, right.' He snorted. 'Look, I know he comes off as Mr Cool, but when you live with him you can sense the disapproval radiating off him. Nothing got said, but there was this constant aura of disappointment, you know?'

He stared at his empty coffee cup. 'I don't know what he expected—that we'd be brilliant at something, I suppose, like him.

'Anyway, it got to me. I started doing drugs big time, using and dealing when I was at school and even more after. Juliana came to me one day in the holidays and asked me for something to give her a thrill. She was bored shitless but she was a great actress. She wanted the excitement of doing something she shouldn't. I gave her some E. That was the day she disappeared.

'I got bombed out of my mind when that happened. Before, when she got a bit low sometimes, she'd talked about swimming right across the harbour and fuck the sharks. I was sure she'd tried it after taking the stuff and drowned.'

'But you didn't say anything?'

He slurped the rest of the coffee. 'How could I? I'd have been in all sorts of shit, not only for causing her death but for the drugs as well, and I was in with some rough people by then. If the cops forced me to give them up . . .'

'I get the picture and it fits certain things that've happened since. But that's not what you're so freaked about now, is it?'

He shook his head and used his tongue to hoik a bit of his beard into his mouth, where he chewed at it with his stained teeth.

'I took on a consignment of ice to sell on commission and I was hijacked when I was wasted. These people want their money and they're going to hurt me really badly if they don't get it.'

'It's a familiar story,' I said. 'But I don't see what it has to do with Juliana.'

'That's it.' He leaned forward so that I could catch the mingled stink of his breath, his body odour and the fear coming off him. 'I sort of cleaned myself up a bit and moved around here and there seeing if I could scare up some action that would make me some money. Enough to . . . you know.'

'Buy time.'

'Yeah, right. Well, one night this chick approached me and said she'd heard I was looking to do business and she could put me in the way of something big. Some stuff coming in that needed storing and cutting and distributing to people who weren't the usual users. Moneyed people.'

'And you weren't looking as crap then as you do now?'

'Right. But it was more than that. She said she knew about me and mentioned one of my mates. She was different, like bigger and darker, lots of makeup, short hair, tatts.' He touched his nose and lower lip. 'Piercings, and a different voice, but I'll swear she was Juliana.'

20

Foxy said he was gobsmacked and wondered if all the drugs he'd used had messed his brain. He didn't feel able to tell her who he thought she was but he believed it, foggy brain or not.

'She called herself Trudi.'

It was an extraordinary story and I felt I needed to get a better handle on it.

'What did you feel when you decided you knew her?'

'Feel?'

'Come on, it's your sister who's thought to be dead. You must have felt something.'

He reached into his pocket for his pills and this time I let him take some. He had the shakes.

'You ever been addicted?' he asked.

'No. Pretty heavily dependent on alcohol, I suppose, but that's it.'

'Addiction doesn't leave much room for feelings, Mr Hardy. Wants and needs take their place. A useless counsellor I once spoke to told me that.'

I waited while the pills brought his shakes under control. With his last remark I had to credit him with an intelligence that hadn't been very obvious before. The name was the key, even if his behaviour hadn't convinced me that he was telling the truth as far as he was able to recognise it.

When he was composed he said, 'You'd expect me to feel guilt about giving her the E and lying to my father and the police, or maybe relieved that she wasn't dead after all, but I didn't feel those things. When I got over the surprise I just worried about what trouble there was for me if it all came out.'

'Okay, I understand. So she had a drug scheme that could get you out of the shit. What did you say to that?'

'I said I was interested, which was true.'

'And?'

'She said it was all being set up and would start smallish but get bigger and that I should meet her again in a week to get rolling.'

'When was this?'

'Two days ago.'

'What happened then?'

'I started thinking and I started back on the pills and other stuff. I was very confused. I thought about steering her to these other people I'm in hock to as a way of getting clear but I decided I couldn't do that.'

'Because she's your sister?'

He laughed. 'Still looking for my better side? You won't fucking find it. No, I got word that the people who ripped me off were the same as the ones who'd supplied me and that they were just double-dipping, so I figured they might do the same to Trudi . . . Juliana, and I'd be no better off.'

I hadn't ever dealt with anyone quite like him before. Most criminals lack empathy, like Foxy, but unlike him they have limited imaginations and a reduced capacity to anticipate the consequences of their actions. Just as well, or they'd be suffering the horrors this boy was suffering. Being intelligent, he knew the dangers but also hadn't quite run out of strategies. At this point, no doubt with the aid of the drugs, he'd pulled himself together.

'I came up with a plan,' he said.

'I'd be interested to hear it.'

'My father once offered a reward of a quarter of a million to find Juliana. Then he hired detectives and you and your kind don't come cheap. That means there's money available for Juliana's . . . safe return. Right?'

I nodded.

'You advance enough of that money for me to get clear of the heavies and I'll arrange for you to meet Trudi and you can carry her home to doting Daddy and Stepmummy, who hates her and is out of her fucking mind on occult shit anyway.'

'How much?'

'Eight grand, give or take.'

'I can do that.'

'I thought so. There's one more thing.'

'There always is.'

'You have to provide the protection when I make the pay-off to my people.'

Foxy thought he had me where he wanted me and to a degree he did, but I wasn't going to allow him to be too complacent.

I pointed a finger at him. 'You don't know enough about what Juliana's been doing. The man she's teamed up with is a long time law-breaker of one kind or another and more than likely a murderer. I have to wonder how he'd feel about your part in turning Juliana in for money. He seems to be obsessed with her. He's resourceful and very protective.'

He looked concerned but quickly recovered. 'Well, you'd just have to protect me from him as well.'

'Why would I do that? With Juliana back home I'm finished. You'd be on your own.'

'Yeah, it's something to think about. Maybe I should get Dad to . . . but I need the immediate problem resolved. I need some money now and a safe place to stay. You get my buy-out money and see me right through that fucking nightmare and then you'll get to meet up with Juliana and cash in with Gerard, and I'll . . . make travel plans.'

'If I agree, and it works out that way, you're going to have to keep your nerve. You need to clean up.'

He nodded. 'I'm trying. Just using the pills, nothing harder, and trying to cut down.'

I studied him and decided he wasn't a completely lost cause. There were good genes in play potentially but genes are unreliable when it comes to a test of character. I realised suddenly that I was more deeply involved in the affairs of the Fonteyn family than I'd anticipated. A concerned but emotionally ill-equipped father, a damaged son, a wayward daughter and a crazy wife and stepmother. It all made my other missing persons cases seem simple.

I levered myself stiffly up from the table where I'd been sitting for too long.

'Okay, Foxy,' I said. 'You're on. Let's go.'

'I have to ask something else,' he said. 'Please don't call me Foxy.'

Over the years, working for lawyers, I've had to stash witnesses away safely. I used the University Motel and the Rooftop Motel, both in Glebe, until the first closed down and the other came under new management unhappy with the arrangement. Lately I'd worked out a system with the manager of a set of serviced apartments in Forest Lodge that was flexible about names and ID. As long as the lawyers paid the bill promptly and the guests behaved themselves there was no trouble.

Foster had been staying with a friend in Darlinghurst. I drove him to collect his belongings and then to the apartments, where I checked him in as Charles Foster. I drew seven hundred and fifty dollars for him from the ATM at my bank and had him wait while I made arrangements to withdraw the larger amount when I required it to bail him out of his difficulty. Then I walked with him back down Wigram Road to Forest Lodge. We both needed the exercise.

'This is going to be tough for you,' I said, 'just waiting and thinking.'

'I know.'

'So go to the movies at the Broadway Centre, watch Foxtel, play games on your phone and laptop and keep your head down while you make the deal. When, d'you think?'

'You can get the money tomorrow?'

'Right.'

'The following night.'

'Where and when?'

'Up to them.'

'Roughly speaking.'

'Bondi maybe, or Clovelly or Coogee. Around there, and late.'

'Let me know as soon as you can and give me an idea of who and how many.'

He swallowed nervously. 'You've done this sort of thing before?'

'Similar, a few times.'

'How'd they work out?'

'Some good, some bad.'

'Thanks a lot.'

'I told you you'd have to keep your nerve.'

'I will.'

I left him standing in the Crescent across from the apartment block that was part of the development that had sprung up where the Harold Park Paceway used to be. He looked small and frightened but was aiming for big and brave. Marks for trying.

21

I rang Hank and said I was going to need some backup.

'Bit of a non-event last time,' he said. 'Any chance of seeing some action?'

'I hope there won't be any,' I said.

'You know what I mean. Just being out and about gets the juices running.'

I told him I'd fill him in when I had the details. I wasn't too concerned. Eight thousand dollars isn't a lot of money in the drug world and I doubted the people Foster was dealing with would be seriously heavy. Since there wouldn't be any drugs changing hands it wouldn't be too risky a meeting to be at. But with drug people you never know and it depended on how truthful Foster had been.

I spent the rest of that day tidying things up. I paid the slightly overdue mortgage payment on the house and some credit card bills—all online, all painless. When you had to reach into your pocket, or even when you had to write a cheque, there was more reality to your financial circumstances, more connection between what you had and what you owed. In the digital age that connection had broken down a bit— good if you were flush, dangerous if you weren't.

With a few drinks inside me I played some early Elvis— 'That's All Right', 'Mystery Train', 'Blue Suede Shoes'—to put me in touch with my youth and its simpler realities.

At least, I thought, the upcoming Foster Fonteyn transaction involved cold, hard cash.

The call came halfway through the next morning.

'Barden Park in Coogee,' Foster said. 'The Green Street gate. D'you know it?'

'No.'

'Neither do I. Hang on.' He used his mobile in the expert way they all can and said he'd found a photo. 'I suppose it's as good as anywhere. It's 11.30 tomorrow night.'

'How many bodies?'

'I don't know. He didn't say and I was too nervous to ask.'

'You know him, the person you spoke to?'

'Not really. We've only dealt by phone and text and courier. He calls himself Jake. I admit I'm scared, Hardy.'

'That's good. Jake'll like that and you should be scared.'

'What do we do?'

'Get there early. I'll pick you up at ten. Are you straight?'

'Straight enough.'

'You better be. Get some exercise today, tire yourself out and have a good night's sleep. Do you have any health problems other than the drugs—asthma, night blindness . . .?'

'No. Why?'

'Just asking. Call me tomorrow if you run into any trouble.'

'What kind of trouble?'

'Any kind.'

I ended the call. I wanted to keep him on edge, not so much as to push him back into his drug refuge but enough to keep him dependent, despite the bargaining chip he was holding, and convinced that his best interests lay in being straight with me, now and from now on.

I rang Hank and gave him the drum. I rang the bank and arranged to draw the cash that afternoon. Then I took my own advice—I did a long, serious workout at the gym and subjected myself to one of Wesley Scott's more vigorous rub-downs.

'Bit of tension here and there, my man,' Wes said.

'It's worldwide.'

'You know what I mean. For a man your age, with your history, your weight's good and the muscle tone is fine. Heart rhythm sounds right.'

He dug his fingers into the strip of muscle running up to the neck from the shoulders I'd built up with the machine over the years. 'Tightness there.'

'It's where I start my thinking,' I said. 'And I have some real thinking to do.'

He slapped me the way he does to indicate that he'd finished.

'Having a party soon to celebrate twenty years. Do you good to come.'

'If everything I've got on hand works out I'll come and I'll do the bloody limbo.'

He laughed. 'Not while I'm your trainer you won't.'

I drove to Coogee the next day to check Barden Park over. It occupied a half-acre corner block and was mostly scruffy grass that looked as if it was a dog exercise area. There was an avenue of trees along one side, gums and Moreton Bay figs, and a path between them running to gateposts at the Green Street exit. The gateposts were a handsome sandstone set about shoulder high.

A few blocks back from the beach, the area featured houses that mostly had driveways. At a guess the street lights would be shrouded by trees at the Green Street end. Ideal for a quick hello-and-goodbye clandestine exchange. I had something a little more than that in mind.

I drove down to the landscaped, sculptured foreshore and parked. It was a much rougher vista in my Maroubra youth when we'd come here after late-afternoon surfing a bit to the south to drink beer and make a nuisance of ourselves. Innocent nuisance it seems now after the politically and racially charged events of recent years.

Now the area was quiet, ideal for roller-bladers, and family friendly.

Back in Glebe I drew out the money. Eighty one-hundred-dollar notes make a fair chunk and would take some time to count. I prepared the things I wanted to take to the meeting—a torch, my .38 Smith & Wesson revolver, cleaned and loaded. I filled in the time finishing Macklin's book on Norfolk, watching Richard E. Grant's movie *Wah-Wah* and eating whatever I could scratch up from the fridge until it was time to collect Foster and Hank.

Foster was nervy but there was no smell of booze or marijuana or even of tobacco.

'Off the fags?' I said as he scrambled into the back seat of the Falcon.

'They say if you can kick the smokes you can kick anything.'

'The thing about quitting is that it's interesting enough in itself to see you through for a while. When that wears off it gets harder. I didn't have much trouble with the smokes, but the times I've had to give up drinking it seemed to apply.'

'Thank you, Counsellor Hardy. I'll add that to the other helpful hints I've been given.'

I let the sarcasm pass; he was young and under a lot of pressure and I had been more than a bit supercilious.

Hank was waiting outside the Newtown flat where he lived with Megan. He got in beside me, sliding in smoothly without apparent effort. Hank was a big man with four or five centimetres on me. He'd played top-level basketball in his US high school and could move like a cat. I introduced them.

'This is Hank, Foster. Hank, this is Foster Fonteyn who's got himself into some shit we're going to get him out of.'

The two exchanged nods and grunts.

'Buy me out of,' Foster said.

'Right.'

The money was a bulge in the deep pocket of the jacket I was wearing.

'Everybody gets paid. Here's what we're going to do.'

I filled them in on precisely how I wanted the thing to go down as we negotiated the late-night traffic to Coogee. We arrived half an hour before the appointed time. Foster and I took up a position near the gateposts where there was just enough light from the street for us to be seen. Hank was only a metre away behind a huge Moreton Bay fig.

The residents in the surrounding houses had settled down for the night. At twenty-five past eleven an SUV appeared. Moving slowly, it cruised along the streets bordering two sides of the park before stopping near a fence across from where we were waiting. Two men got out: one big, one a lot smaller.

Both paused to light cigarettes, then the big one stepped easily over the fence and the smaller one had to scramble a bit. They walked towards us across the grass to the path we were on. They had to pass the big tree and Hank stepped out and took the big man down in a bone-crunching tackle. I grabbed the other man and put the .38 hard into the soft flesh beside his jawbone. He yelped and dropped his cigarette, flicking up sparks.

'Stomp on that,' I said to Foster. 'We don't want a fire, now do we?'

Foster did as he was told. I backed my man hard up against the stone gatepost, keeping the pistol biting into him. Hank had his man down on his belly with a knee on his back and had both his arms pinned.

I handed the torch to Foster. 'Show him the money.'

He took it out of my pocket. His hands were trembling and he almost dropped it but he managed to switch on the torch and light up the package. I eased the pistol away.

'Are you Jake?'

He nodded.

'Well, Jake, you see how things are. You take the money and you and this man are quits for good. Do you understand?'

He gulped and nodded.

'You don't contact him. You don't sic anyone onto him. Not now, not ever. Got it?'

Another nod.

I stepped back. 'Give him the money.'

Foster handed the bundle of notes over and I took a photo of the moment with my phone while still keeping the .38 in play. In the flash Jake looked like a frightened rabbit, red-eyed with his mouth slack and open.

'I don't care who you are, Jake, or who you might be working for. If this man has any trouble I come looking for you and you won't like what I do to you. Now take your money, tell your mate to behave himself and piss off.'

He scrambled away clutching the money. Hank let his man up slowly and he limped away with Jake muttering to him. Hank joined us and dusted off the knee of his pants.

'No worries,' he said.

I put the pistol back in its holster under my arm. 'We'll make an Aussie of you yet.'

Foster jerked nervously at the sound of the SUV revving unnecessarily before driving away.

'You all right?' I asked.

He nodded.

The whole thing had taken barely five minutes.

22

I dropped Hank in Newtown. I thanked him and Foster had the grace to thank him as well. He was improving. We went up to his apartment and he made coffee. He didn't have any alcohol there and, he insisted, no drugs.

'Think you can stay off the drugs?'

'I'll need help.'

'That shouldn't be hard to find. How long since you spoke to your father?'

He shrugged. 'I'm not sure. Weeks. I try to avoid speaking to him if I can.'

'I like your father. He's trusted me further than any client I remember. Of course, he has the financial resources but it was more than that. We saw eye to eye along the way.'

'I bet you haven't told him the latest.'

'No, not yet. I'm tossing up when to do it. I take your

point that he made demands on his children that were unreasonable and damaging. He'll have to face that.'

'You think he can? Think you can make him?'

'We'll see. To answer your question, I don't want to watch another family disintegrate in front of me partly because of my actions. I've seen it too often. I want this to go smoothly and for everyone to be a survivor. Understand?'

He nodded but looked very uncertain.

'What?' I said.

He'd showered and trimmed his beard neat and kept his hair clean. I wouldn't have been surprised to find tooth-whitening gunk in the bathroom along with underarm deodorant and nail-cleaning equipment. He was trying to hold a line but something was troubling him. It'd be a matter of his strength of character whether he admitted what it was or tried a cover-up. He took a deep breath.

'Hardy,' he said. 'I . . .'

'Spit it out, son. You've got my attention.'

'I was still high when I met her in the pub and pretty freaked when I first spoke to you. Now I'm clean or getting there . . . I don't know . . . the world looks different.'

'What're you saying?'

'Now, I'm not a hundred and ten per cent sure it was Juliana.'

He collapsed then; the strain of what he'd been going through had stretched him too far. I lifted him onto the couch, surprised at how light he was, and made him comfortable.

His breathing was shallow but regular and his eyes were open. I got him some water and pulled a chair close to sit near him.

'I'm sorry,' he said.

'Don't worry. Feel up to talking?'

'Yeah.'

I had Cameron's photograph of the girl on the jetty in Norfolk Island folded in my wallet with the image untouched by the folds. I took it out and showed it to him.

'That's Juliana!'

'I think so. But is she the girl you met?'

'Oh, shit, yes . . . I'm not sure.'

'Let's see if I can help. She was drinking, right?'

'Bloody Marys.'

'I could do with one right now. Was she sitting opposite you?'

He nodded.

'Right, now think back. Which hand did she drink with?'

He closed his eyes, running the mental video. 'The left.'

'Did she have any tatts?'

'Shit, yes. But they looked pretty recent—she kept rubbing one of them the way you do.'

'You mentioned a piercing?'

He was right back in the scene now. 'God, you're good. She worked at a lower lip ring with her tongue all the time.'

'I can tell you that girl in the photograph, the one I've

been tracking, calls herself Trudi. I think we've got some pretty good confirmation here. Enough to proceed anyway.'

'Proceed how?'

I got up. 'I'm going to have to think about it. Three nights till you're meeting with her, right?'

He nodded.

'No communication beforehand?'

He shook his head. 'I asked for her mobile number but she said she didn't have one. I asked her to call me but she said she couldn't.'

I nodded. 'Harris wouldn't give her that independence.'

'She's in danger then?'

I judged it was time to jolt him again.

'What do you care?'

He was wrung out. He pressed his fingers into his eyes and let them slide down his cheeks. 'I do care.'

'Good. It's another waiting game, Foster. What you have to do is keep yourself straight. Can you swim?'

'Of course I can swim.'

'Go to Victoria Park pool and lap till you drop. The City Gym's just down the way . . .'

'I don't think so.'

'Well, the university's there as well. Walk around, look at the buildings, have coffee, find someone to chat to, read stuff in the library. Fill your day.'

'What'll you be doing?'

'Thinking, thinking hard.'

'I still haven't told you where and when I'm supposed to meet her. And you haven't asked.'

'I'm trusting you to tell me when I need to know.'

I went home, slept poorly and woke up unrefreshed and grouchy. The way ahead seemed straightforward—be present when Foster met his sister and let them play out whatever way it went. Then follow the girl to somewhere she could be talked to, possibly with her father present. I still hadn't decided on that. With Hank as backup I felt I could handle Harris. If I was past my best, probably so was he with booze and drugs and years of ducking for cover. But I had a strong feeling I was missing something that could stuff all this up. Another gym session didn't help. A good evening with Megan, Hank and the boys did a bit. I handed over the *Bounty* items which, even though they were fakes, were well-made and worked. But the nagging feeling stayed with me.

I spoke to Foster a few times and felt confident he was playing his part according to my script. The day before he was due to meet 'Trudi' all my misgivings took solid shape. I was considering whether to contact Fonteyn when the doorbell rang and I opened the door to a familiar face.

'Hello, Hardy,' George D'Amico said.

I nodded and ushered him in. He wore one of his impeccable suits with a dark shirt and slightly lighter tie, very modish.

We went down the passage to the living room, where he gave the fittings an indifferent glance before sitting down.

'You've been busy,' he said.

'So've you, apparently.'

'Not so much. I have contacts in the drug scene, as you can imagine, and money buys information. I'm told you pulled young Foxy Foster Fonteyn out of a sticky situation the other night. Well done.'

'Cut the bullshit, George. Why're you here?'

He looked around the room. 'Is this the best you can afford? No security, basic amenities? You're not doing much better than Vaughan Turnbull was, but I hear that you financed him for a holiday, so I concluded that you have resources.'

'You like the sound of your own voice, don't you?'

He laughed. 'I guess you're right. The thing is, knowing you had money to spend and picking up the name Fonteyn from the druggies, it didn't take long to figure out the case you were on and what progress you've made.'

'Keep enjoying yourself.'

'You're beginning to irritate me but that's what you're trying to do so I'll resist it. You're protecting the brother of a girl missing from a wealthy family. I'm told he's a useless bit of shit so I'm guessing you're hoping to use him to help you find her and cash in.'

'Let's say for argument's sake that you're right. What's your interest?'

'Just one—Harris. You give me Harris and you can do what you like with the girl. Cash her in big time.'

I shook my head. 'That's you all over, George. You see people as commodities; it's sleazy and sort of boring. No deal.'

He flushed. 'I should've put you overboard when I had the chance.'

'Then you wouldn't be as close on Harris's trail as you seem to think you are.'

I didn't have air-conditioning; the room was warm and he was sweating. I was in shirtsleeves and D'Amico was in a jacket and tie. He took a handkerchief from his inside breast pocket and wiped his brow.

'Okay, I understand. Look, you're right and Paul was right. All that about the young girls was a mistake, especially . . .'

I laughed. 'You're a bit late. Have the enquiries into child molestation spooked you? Wouldn't be good to go inside as a rock spider.'

He struggled not to lose his composure again. 'For what it's worth I never employed underage girls. They were all sixteen plus, I had them checked out, for Christ's sake, and they were never my personal taste.'

I shrugged. 'Checks can be unreliable. Suppose a couple slipped through the net and want to talk, looking for compensation?'

'I can bugger your plans completely, Hardy. All I have to do is contact the father and tell him what's happening.

I'm guessing you haven't done that. You're too much of a fucking show-pony. But I'd rather do a deal with you.'

He was right that him talking to Fonteyn, with whatever spin he chose to put on his information, would create a problem, but there was more to say. The trade-offs were getting tricky.

I took him upstairs to my office. I'd had Cameron transfer the photo of Desiree to my phone and I'd incorporated it into the Fonteyn file on my computer. I called up the file and turned the screen towards him with the image loading.

'What's this?'

'Take a look. I don't do deals with people who murder women.'

He squinted across the desk and then reached into his jacket for a glasses case. He hooked on a pair of elegant wire-rimmed spectacles he was usually too vain to wear and peered at the screen. His expression was hard to read. It certainly wasn't shock—more like reluctant acceptance.

He took off the glasses and fiddled with them. 'I didn't do this.'

'Who did? Serge?'

'No. If I tell you will you consider my proposition?'

Vaughan Turnbull must have been one of the last people to see Desiree alive and he was working with my money. He'd admit that if questioned; I didn't want any involvement with the woman's murder and even having the photograph was dangerous.

'Convince me and I might just think about it.'

He sighed and suddenly looked a bit older and bit less svelte. 'Rafa,' he said. 'Fucking Senior Sergeant Raffaello Cantini.'

23

D'Amico loosened his tie and took off his jacket. When he was comfortable he told me that his brother Paul had been Desiree's lover, in defiance of every bit of advice he'd offered.

'She was still attached to Harris, even though they were divorced. Paul was convinced that the kid she'd had was his and not Harris's. The kid was parked with Desiree's mother in Brisbane. Desiree wouldn't confirm or deny it and it drove Paul crazy.

'Cantini's a relative and as you might have gathered, he looks after certain of our interests. He was ashamed of Paul's . . . obsession with that hooker. When Paul was killed Cantini went to her to try and locate Harris to square the ledger and things . . . went wrong. Rafa's pretty crazy.'

'Cantini told you this?'

'No, his wife did. She's my sister. She's worried about his mental health.'

'Not to mention his criminal activities.'

'That'll be worked out. The point is I didn't kill the woman. And that takes care of your objection about helping me give Harris what he fucking deserves.'

'I'll have to think about it.'

'Think fast. I can screw you up real good by tying you to Desiree's killing through Vaughan. I'd have no trouble finding a witness to say he saw you at the houseboat.'

He turned in his seat and took a pen and a card from his jacket that was getting creased on the back of the chair. He wrote down some figures in a big looping hand on the card that named him as the representative of some sort of sporting goods business and flipped it towards me.

'My number. You work out what you're going to do about grabbing the girl and you tell me. Then we fucking cooperate.'

He stood, hooked up his jacket and left the room. I followed him down the stairs and out the door. He was adjusting his clothes as he went and would've been close to his immaculate self when he reached the street. He lifted his hand and a silver Mercedes purred up. He got in without looking back.

For all his polish, George D'Amico was just a flashy hood for my money and there was no way I was going to help him garotte Lance Harris or deep-six him, or do whatever else he had in mind. He'd forced my hand but that was all he'd done and he didn't know a thing about it.

*

I phoned Gerard Fonteyn and arranged to meet him at his office that afternoon, giving me time to assemble some photos, voice records and my thoughts. I found twenty minutes to go to a café, eat a sandwich and wash down my medications with a white wine spritzer. I was increasingly playing fast and loose with the meds, because I'd recently been having misgivings about their side-effects and I knew I'd have to come to a decision about the regime soon.

Fonteyn hadn't even asked me why I wanted the meeting. His faith in me was almost embarrassing and I had to hope what I'd tell him wouldn't dent it too much. I was escorted to his office immediately on my arrival and, after greeting me, Fonteyn announced to the employee, a businesslike thirtyish woman, that he wasn't to be interrupted for anything short of a nuclear attack. She smiled and left us.

'It's a long story and not a very pleasant one,' I said.

'I have just one question before you start—is she alive?'

'I'm ninety-nine per cent sure she is.'

'Go on.'

I gave him the latest, chapter and verse. He was composed throughout, comfortable in his shirtsleeves with air-conditioning keeping the big room at an agreeable temperature. His expression tightened a few times when I referred to his children's resentment of his expectations, and to their drug-taking. And, at a guess, he didn't think much of tattoos and body piercing; but he was in the cosmetics business and must have been aware they were fashionable.

Both were correctable anyway, as he would know. Fonteyn was the sort of confident man whose life experience had taught him that things could be put right. I was relying on that.

When I'd finished he leaned back in his chair and waggled his fingers, an oddly frivolous gesture for him. 'As I get older,' he said, 'I find a drink or two sort of loosens the knots in the brain when I have a problem. What d'you think about that, Cliff?'

'I agree—one or two, as you say.'

He produced a bottle of cognac and two glasses from a deep drawer in his desk and we moved to the comfortable chairs. No toast. Just an exchange of nods and we drank.

'Would you have told me everything if this D'Amico hadn't threatened to disrupt your plans? Not that I know what your plans are.'

Typically acute of Fonteyn, that question. 'I had trouble deciding.'

'Do you believe that he only wants Harris and has no interest in Juliana?'

'It's possible. On the other hand, he might consider that she was implicated in the death of his brother, or he might think to seize the opportunity to extort money from you now he's found out who she is and knows that she comes from money. It'd show.'

Fonteyn winced. 'Therefore it's imperative that he be kept ignorant of where and when Foster is to meet . . . this Trudi.'

'That's right.'

The cognac was slipping down smoothly. Fonteyn said, 'You're very protective of Foster. You could have pressured him.'

'He's very fragile, potentially volatile, and already under a lot of strain. Any more might crack him. I should tell you my idea is simply to get hold of the girl by physical force if need be and get her back for you to deal with. To bring that off, Foster will have to hold his nerve and play his part. As I've told you, he did pretty well the other night and I need him in that frame of mind.'

The drink didn't seem to be helping Fonteyn. He pushed his glass away. 'We're talking about my children but I feel as if they're people I don't know. Why not tell the police when you know the time and venue? Have the place surrounded and . . . overwhelm the situation?'

'Do you think I'm trying to hog the glory?'

'No, no, I didn't mean . . .'

'I wouldn't have blamed you, but it's not quite like that. Lance Harris is using the girl as his advance guard. Foster encouraged her to think he could be useful in marketing the drugs Harris has got hold of somewhere along the line. Maybe on tick, pending the sale of his boat. But Harris is an experienced drug dealer and general outlaw. When Juliana goes to meet Foster he'll be super-alert for signs of interference. Put enough cops in there and he'll spot them and abort the whole thing before it even starts.'

'It sounds as if you know what you're talking about.'

'Not precisely, but in broad terms, yes. And something else: if I went to the police and convinced them, which isn't certain anyway, Foster and Juliana end up as druggies and the story explodes in the media. You've trusted me, and what I want in return is for you and yours to come out of this clean. You'll have a hell of a big job on your hands then.'

He tossed off his cognac. 'That's true. All right, what am I to do?'

I'd made up my mind. 'A hard thing—just wait and hope.'

He nodded. 'Do you need more money?'

'No, there's been too much money washing around already. Remember the deal about the interview with your daughter, though. That has to hold.'

He nodded. 'Thank you.'

'Too soon for that,' I said.

I'd watched for a tail ever since I left the office, thinking D'Amico might be interested in where I went and who I saw. But he was out of his territory and probably didn't have the manpower, which was a comfort. When I was sure I was clear I drove to the Forest Lodge apartments intending to reassure Foster that his father was aware of what was happening and understood that he had to change as much as Foster did. Unless all filial feeling had gone I thought this would bolster Foster's confidence and resolve.

I parked and buzzed the apartment. No answer. Then I rang Foster's mobile and was informed that it was out of service. I'd told him to keep it charged. The manager of the apartments lived on site and buzzed me in. He met me in the lobby.

'Hi, Cliff? What's up?'

Joe Chambers was an old Glebe resident who claimed to have played tennis there with Lew Hoad as a boy. He'd inherited the house where the apartments now stood and had been happy to accept the offer of a large flat and to take on the management as part of the deal for selling to a developer. He was Glebe old school, remembering the days when publicans kept a club under the bar, which was why he'd welcomed the arrangement with me.

'Gidday, Joe. Seen anything of my guy lately?'

'I have, you know. He brought a young bloke back with him after one of his walks and they went up to his room for a while and then they left together.'

'What sort of young bloke?'

'That's it. Your Charlie Foster was really smartening himself up. New clothes and I'd say a spring in his step. But this bloke was a real scruff with that look, you know?'

'What look, Joe?'

'I'd say he was stoned when he arrived and that they were both stoned when they left. I'm sorry, Cliff, I'm not a nursemaid.'

24

Joe let me in to Foster's apartment and the signs were all there—the place reeked of marijuana smoke and there were roaches in a saucer. There was the wrapping for a six-pack of Jim Beam and cola and a crumpled pill foil. There was also a folded sheet of notepaper with my name scrawled across it. I put it in my pocket.

'Sorry, Joe. I thought he was on the mend.'

'Not your fault, it happens, but it's a pain in the arse. Reckon he'll be back?'

'I hope so. I'd be glad if you'd let me know if he shows up.'

Joe wasn't happy but he agreed. I told him I'd settle with him as soon as I knew what was happening. He wanted to know what the note said but he could see from my attitude that I wasn't going to tell him.

'Have to air this place out,' he grunted. 'And it looks like they've spilled booze on the carpet here and there.'

'Leave it till I know more. I'll pay for the cleaning.'

That mollified him slightly even if it didn't satisfy his curiosity. He stalked out of the flat and we parted on terms very different from the way we'd started. That was a worry for the future but not as much as the thought of Foster out drifting around in what I wouldn't be surprised if the media started calling the 'drug community'.

It was raining and I got wet getting back to the car. It didn't help my mood. Sitting damply behind the wheel I unfolded the note. The looped writing had ignored the lines, cases and punctuation, and the paper had a brown stain in one corner.

cliff sorry couldn't face her or gerard or you tried but fucked up beer garden waverley hotel tomorrow night 10 good luck foster

It could've been worse. He might have just gone up in smoke without a trace, but it left me some serious worries. One was Foster himself. There was despair in the few scrawled words and people who went back onto drugs after even a short drying out often overdosed.

Suddenly, much of what I'd said to Gerard Fonteyn no longer held true. I'd implied that Foster was safe and that I had a straightforward plan. Foster wasn't safe. He had an enemy in Jake of Coogee and George D'Amico. If D'Amico got hold of Foster through his drug contacts—

possible if not probable—and forced him to talk, there went my plan.

Through the rest of the day and most of the day following I kept trying to contact Foster with no success. He hadn't come back to Forest Lodge and I had no idea who his bad Samaritan was. I drove to the Double Bay café where I'd seen him but learned nothing.

I filled Hank in on what had happened and he appreciated the seriousness of it.

'The only thing I can think to do,' I said, 'is show up myself. I know what she looks like and the background. I might be able to persuade her to . . .'

'Dump her boyfriend and her new, exciting life? That'd be pushing it uphill, Cliff.'

I tried to imagine the scene. We had to assume Harris was scoping the meeting place but would he turn up with the girl? He must know that George D'Amico would be looking for him so he'd need to lie low. He'd also know how unreliable drug negotiations can be with no one knowing quite what pressures the other party might be under. My guess would be that he'd be nearby but not at the meeting. Even if he was there I felt sure Hank could handle him. My problem would be to talk fast and well enough to get her to break with Harris. Would it help to talk about her brother? Would it make a difference to tell her that people, including her father, knew who she was and that she needed protection from George D'Amico and the law for her association with the man who killed Paul D'Amico?

It was thin ice—banking on both D'Amico and Harris being out of the immediate picture. But it was the only thing to do: play with the cards I held. I rang Colin Cameron.

The Waverley hotel was in Bronte, well back from the beach but elevated so that it afforded views of the water from the beer garden and a pretty good glimpse of the Waverley Cemetery, where a good deal of Sydney history was buried. I learned this from the hotel's website, which made everything look very glossy, although I suspect it concealed a certain amount of the inevitable wear and tear from the salty air and corrosive winds.

The beer garden was the traditional set-up with an entrance through the hotel but also up a flight of steps from the street. Easiest way in, easiest way out. Benches, tables, chairs and umbrellas and private nooks shielded by head-high trees in big wooden garden boxes. The website provided day and night views and it looked as though the subtle lighting out in the after-dark beer garden could allow all sorts of things to go on. Whoever had chosen it, Harris presumably, knew his stuff. That didn't raise my confidence.

Hank and I arrived forty-five minutes before the appointed time. Cameron turned up in a taxi a few minutes later. I made the introductions and we went over the moves. My job was to identify the girl as soon as she appeared, approach her and persuade her to talk to me.

'Sorry, Cliff,' Hank said, 'but what's Colin here for?'

That was Hank, covering all the bases. Cameron looked sober and composed.

'Colin's been involved since the beginning,' I said. 'He's got a sort of right to be here, an investment, as it were.'

Hank studied Cameron in his shorts, flapping sports shirt, baseball cap and heavy glasses. Being an expert in such things himself, he noticed the miniature camera in Cameron's shirt pocket and nodded.

'Colin's going to show her the photo he took of her on Norfolk Island and the one of the woman who was killed up in Coolangatta. The idea is to scare her if my initial spiel doesn't work.'

'And if she runs?'

'We follow her.'

We drifted in, Hank and me first and Cameron a bit behind us. He went straight to the bar. Hank and I positioned ourselves where we could easily be seen by anyone coming in through either entrance.

It was mid-week and the pub was only doing fair business inside and out. There were about twenty tables and five benches, all half-occupied. Possibly a third of the patrons were women and at least half of them were smoking, but many fewer men were. The way it is. The music out there was muted, the way it should be.

Cameron returned with a schooner and started doing things on his phone. Hank got a bottle of white wine and we waited. The time ticked by. The appointed time came and went. If anything was going to happen it was going to be late. How late? I checked my watch out of the corner of my eye.

A shadow fell across the table as a tall, broad-shouldered man came close. He wore a silk shirt, a loose linen jacket and stone-washed jeans and all he needed to be a stand-in for the mature Errol Flynn was for his dark hair to be more slicked back and the moustache to be more clipped.

He sat. 'Hello, Hardy,' he said. 'I'm Lance Harris. Who's your friend?'

25

Harris produced an empty wine glass with the flourish of a conjurer. He poured himself a solid belt of white and raised the glass.

'Don't look so surprised, Hardy. Blokes like you leave a trail behind them and people love to talk. Or can be made to talk.'

Harris was a quite well-preserved fifty or a dissipated forty. Just the beginnings of jowls and the neck scrawniness that marks the years like the rings on a tree. He was clear-eyed but hadn't hauled hard on too many ropes lately; the loose shirt covered a softening belly.

'Where is she, Harris?' I said.

Harris was unfazed. 'How many people have you got here, Hardy, apart from this big hunk?'

'One more. Enough.'

Harris shook his head and moved, shifting in his seat.

'Not enough by a long way, sport. I've got a .22 popgun here under the table pointed at your essentials, more or less. One silly move from you or Sampson here or a gesture to the other one and you're hurt where it really hurts and I'm gone.'

His voice was steady, he was stone cold sober and I realised too late that he'd used his left hand to pour and handle his drink. He could have been bluffing but the odds were against it.

I put both my hands on the table. 'What do you want, Harris?'

He smiled. 'What we all want—a great big, juicy win, just one. You're in line for it and so am I.'

'When did you find out what she was worth?'

'Before I answer that, tell your friend here to inform the other one what's happening and then they can both piss off.'

'Better do it, Hank,' I said. 'He's holding the cards. I don't think he's as cocksure as he seems; he's got some deal in mind. I'm sorry and I'm embarrassed but I'll have to deal with it myself now.'

Hank said, 'You sure?'

'He's sure,' Harris said. 'Now do as you're told.'

Hank finished his drink and got up. 'Hope to see you again, Mr Harris.'

'I doubt it. Go, Yank, go!'

Hank took his time but eventually he and Cameron left the beer garden. My mobile rang as soon as they'd gone.

'That'll be your Yank mate. Tell him to go home. I don't want to shoot you but I will if I'm interfered with. The stakes are high but it doesn't have to come to that.'

I did as he asked.

Harris nodded. 'Very smart,' he said. 'Now we'll just have a quiet drink and let the air clear.'

He brought his hand up from under the table to show a small, chrome-finish, pearl-handled pistol.

'A lady's gun,' he said, 'but for the sake of your pride I wanted to show you I wasn't bluffing.'

I poured us both some wine. 'How about an answer to a couple of questions?'

He raised an eyebrow stagily. 'A couple, now? Fire away.'

'Why did you have her set up the meeting here with her brother? Was it ever for real?'

'Good question. It was, just for a bit before I worked out who she was and your part in things. I needed some capital.'

'After you found out, why go through with it? Why not just approach me directly?'

He gave a smile, flashing white teeth in a tanned face that had probably helped him with women old and young over the years. 'Call it a sense of the dramatic,' he said. 'And to answer your earlier question, I have to admit it took a while for me to do a bit of research and to decide that this was the best way to go. She made up all sorts of stories and she was pretty convincing. She's very intelligent and she's read a lot and I think she enjoyed fantasising. Had me guessing, I can tell you.'

'What about when you got her stoned?'

'I have to put you right about a few things there, Hardy. In the first place, she didn't look and act like fifteen. Big girl, muscles on her like an Olympic athlete, and she wasn't a virgin either.'

'No?'

'No, and she was no stranger to drugs. She was a mile high on something when I picked her up.'

'I suppose you're going to say you saved her from drowning.'

'No, but maybe from sunstroke and dehydration. She was stark naked on a thirty-five-degree day, drifting on an air mattress with no fucking idea of where she was or what she was doing.'

'So you should have notified the authorities.'

He laughed. 'Me? Authorities? That's about the last thing I'd have done. I'd taken on a load of . . . never mind what, and I was heading off for the wild blue yonder. I had places to go, people to meet, money to make and I'll tell you this—when she got a grip on herself she was happy to come along and she was bloody useful. Could she sail? I'll say she could.'

'But she knows the score now?'

He gave that smile again. 'She knows the whole score.'

'Going to be tough on her.'

'She's resilient, she'll cope.'

I began to get a sense then of the dynamic that had evidently built up between the two, drug-fuelled no doubt, but also with aspects of admiration, perhaps mutual, sex and adventure. I thought back to what Foster had said about the straitjackets high expectation had laced them into and his method of escape.

'Deep in thought, Hardy? That worries me. Share them.'

'Did she really believe Foxy could handle a sizeable drug deal?'

He shrugged. 'Hard to say. He talked big back when they ... he'd been fucking her as soon as the school year ended. I got that straight among all the fantasies. And he gave her the stuff that sent her paddling off to Kirribilli.'

'I know. He told me, but not about the sex.'

'I don't like to boast but I gather he wasn't much good. Anyway, she didn't hold a grudge. Wanted to help the creep, I reckon.'

I had my doubts about that. Harris obviously thought he was smart, playing a role, pretending to be obsessed by her, but what if Juliana was playing a role too?

'Where is she?'

'Not far away. Under restraint.'

'Another serious crime.'

He shrugged. 'I'm a good Samaritan, restoring a lost soul to her family.'

'For a price.'

'Of course.'

'How much?'

'Very reasonable—half a million. Don't worry, I've cleaned her up chemically—she was getting a bit out of control. Anyway, can't charge that amount for damaged goods, not that it's much for the skin-cream king.'

'He's a bit more than that, you might find. If this goes through safely, he'll send people to track you down wherever you go. He's got the resources to do it.'

He almost sneered. 'People like you?'

'No, not like me. I'm too old to go traipsing off to third-world shitholes, which is where you'd have to go, given Fonteyn's money, Interpol and all that.'

'You're making me think of raising the ante.'

'Wouldn't matter.'

'What if I was to approach him directly?'

'You could try, but I'd say that'd treble your risk, quadruple it maybe.'

The level in the bottle had gone down and he lowered it further. I had him a little off-balance now, not a lot, but perhaps enough.

'You're a good talker,' he said, 'but I haven't seen you do much.'

'Before I'd even mention it to Fonteyn I'd have to see and speak to the girl. You weren't bluffing about the gun, but you could be bluffing about her. Who's to say she hasn't slipped away into the druggie twilight or had a . . . chemical accident? Courtesy of you.'

'That's not going to happen, but I take your point. Okay, you can see her.'

'I assume you have someone guarding her?'

'I have, a trusted confederate about the size of your muscle man, so you'd better behave yourself.'

It was the only way I could see to stay in the game so I agreed. At a pinch, given favourable circumstances, I could back myself against two men, always supposing neither was a true professional. Harris was big but running to fat and too sure of himself. As to the other man, big didn't necessarily mean good, or smart.

We left the beer garden and walked to where Harris unlocked a road-weary SUV.

'You drive,' Harris said.

'You're letting me see where she's being held?'

'She's a fucking pawn. She can be moved.'

He was edgy now. I thought about mentioning George D'Amico and Rafa Cantini to keep him that way, but decided to bide my time. He gave me the keys and I started the car. He gave me directions by pointing. He sat stiffly and belched a couple of time.

'Crook innards?' I said.

He didn't reply but kept looking in the rear-vision mirror from time to time. But it takes an expert to spot an expert tail and I was sure Hank would be on the job in the Falcon, to which he and Megan had keys, and that Harris wouldn't see him.

As Harris had said, it wasn't far. We threaded through the

fairly light traffic, made the turns Harris indicated, skirting Bondi Junction, and entered a quiet, tree-shaded street I guessed to be somewhere close to Centennial Park.

'We're here,' he said.

He indicated a corner house with an overgrown garden and I turned the vehicle through open gates down a short, weed-infested gravel driveway.

We got out and I felt the small barrel of the pistol dig into my ribs, harder than was necessary.

'You want to see the girl, right? You can do it with a .22 bullet in your shoulder and I'm thinking about doing it to show her dad how serious I am, and because I don't like you, so move very carefully.'

The air was cool, smelling of decayed vegetation, accumulated rubbish and cat piss. Harris jabbed me again with the pistol but then took it away so that I didn't know where it was. He'd obviously done something like this before. A paved path led from the driveway to steps up to the porch of a tall Federation house.

Harris said, 'Up the steps and open the door. She's in the front room to the right and don't forget about my guy on guard.'

It was dark apart from a trendy fake coachman's lantern with a dim bulb burning over the door. I turned the elaborately designed knob and pushed the door open. After that what happened was very quick, very loud and everything changed completely.

26

One step inside the house and I stumbled into something that had me lurching backwards and bumping into Harris, who fired a shot that was loud in the enclosed space and pinged off a wall. Then he blundered into the same obstacle. We were still only lit by the outside lamp but that was enough to see that a man lay spreadeagled and inert on the floor.

'Jesus!' Harris shouted and in his panic he pointed the gun at me. Next he was grunting as an arm circled his neck and yelping as Hank slammed his hand against the wall, causing him to drop the pistol.

'You all right, Cliff?'

I was crouched by the body. 'Yeah. But this guy's dead. Hold on to Harris and hit him hard if you have to.'

But Harris had slumped down and offered no resistance as he was pushed to the floor into a sitting position with Hank standing over him.

'Who is he?' Hank said.

'Harris had him minding the girl. She was supposed to be in this room here.'

'Dead?' Harris said. 'How?'

'Knife wound to the heart at a guess; there's scarcely any blood at all. Close the door, Hank, and see if you can find a light switch. No prints.'

The door closed quietly and another low-wattage light came on. The door to the room Harris had indicated was ajar and I pushed it open with my elbow. There was just enough light now to see that the room held a narrow bed and a few pieces of basic furniture. There were a couple of empty juice containers and wrappers from chocolate bars. Several heavy, elasticised straps lay on the bed. They'd been sliced through and the cut ends were bloodstained.

'She's gone,' I said to no one in particular. 'What is this place?'

Hank had let Harris stand up and kept close beside him as they looked into the room.

'One of my sainted brother's properties,' Harris said. 'He buys them cheap, pretties them up and sells dear. He's been hanging on to this one till the time was right. I was thinking of burning it down when I'd finished with it but the bugger'd have it insured to the hilt.'

'Brotherly love,' I said.

Hank looked at his watch. 'What now, Cliff?'

Harris sneered. 'Yeah, what now, Cliff?'

Before I could answer my mobile rang.

'Hardy, this is George D'Amico. I've got the girl and I can tell you where Harris is, or where he was until very recently.'

'I know where he is. I've got him right here.'

'Oh, well, that makes things easier. We had to leave there pretty quickly after the wet work, as I'm sure you'll understand.'

Hank and Harris were looking at me enquiringly but I shook my head. 'I understand.'

'Good, now we can arrange a straight swap, Harris for the girl.'

'That's interesting, I . . .'

Hank was gesturing frantically at me and pointing to Harris, who had slumped sideways. In seconds his shirt was sodden, he was sweating so profusely.

D'Amico's voice was almost shrill. 'Hardy?'

'I've got an emergency here. Call again later.'

I cut the call and crouched beside Harris. I immediately recognised the symptoms. I double-checked by looking at his fingertips, which were calloused from testing his blood sugar level.

'He's a diabetic having a hypo from stress and not watching his sugar level. He should have something on him to help.'

We dug into the pockets of his jacket and came up with an opened packet of jelly beans held together with an elastic band. I crammed some into his mouth.

'Chew and swallow, chew and swallow. Suck it down!'

He did and I kept feeding him until he stopped trembling and the sweat stopped breaking out on him.

'We have to get out of here,' I said. 'Where's the Falcon?'

'In the street. Can he walk?'

'Better carry him, he'll be weak for a while.'

Hank lifted Harris without difficulty and we left the room. I picked up Harris's pistol from the passage and looked around to make sure we hadn't left any traces, turned out the light using the butt of the gun and opened the door, wiping the knob with my sleeve. The spent bullet would be someone else's problem. We waited on the porch to make sure all was quiet and then went quickly to the car. With Harris still unresisting, Hank got in the back with him and I drove sedately through the gates and down the silent street.

Hank half carried, half walked Harris into my house and eased him down onto the living-room couch. He was sweating again and I fed him more jelly beans. He gulped them down and leaned back, letting out a low groan. His eyes were closing and I slapped him lightly.

'What's your name?'

'Fuck you. Gotta sleep.'

He stretched out to his full length and wriggled twice, then appeared to fall asleep.

'He going to be all right?' Hank said.

'I think so. Have to watch him. If he's hard to wake in half an hour I'll get my doctor to give him a glucose shot.'

'How do you know all this diabetes stuff?'

'My mother was a diabetic. She'd get on the piss and forget to eat or take too much insulin and go into a hypo. My sister and I pulled her out of them plenty of times.'

'Do they do any damage?'

'Brain damage if you have them often and severely enough.'

'How about your mom?'

'Sharp as a tack until the day she died at eighty-one, despite the booze, the fags and the sugar.'

'Augurs well for you.'

'Maybe. Come out to the kitchen and have a drink. I need to fill you in on what's happening. I don't want him to hear. He might just be faking.'

'Is that likely?'

'People with chronic diseases learn to be cunning. I'll take his shoes and socks off in case he tries to do a runner. He wouldn't get far on that busted-up path of mine.'

I shoved a cushion under Harris's head and we went to the kitchen and I poured us solid slugs of Black Douglas over ice. I told Hank what D'Amico had proposed.

Hank shook his head. 'You can't do that.'

'I know. I have to figure out a way of getting the girl without putting Harris's head in a noose, and . . .'

'And what?'

'At least giving him a chance. Thanks for tonight. You'd better be getting home.'

Hank finished his drink and fished out his mobile to call a cab. We moved back to the living room where Harris was snoring.

Hank said, 'A couple of things—how did D'Amico find where Harris was holding the girl?'

'He didn't say. Maybe Harris was indiscreet about hiring muscle and D'Amico got word somehow.'

'What about the dead guy?'

'I'll call it in anonymously from a public phone.'

He pointed at Harris. 'What're you going to do about him?'

Before I could answer there was a crash and a splintering sound and another crash and the room was full of people— two men with guns shouting for us not to move and George D'Amico holding a tall girl in front of him like a shield.

The two men covered Hank and me. D'Amico let go of the girl, took a pistol from the pocket of his overcoat, took two steps, put the gun to Harris's head and fired. The man covering Hank flinched at the explosion and Hank threw his mobile phone at his head. It hit him; he screamed and his hand swept up to his face.

'My eye! He got my fucking eye.'

The distraction was enough for me to aim a kick at the knee of the other man. It barely connected but threw him off-balance and he lurched against D'Amico, who shoved him away.

A siren wailed, stopped and wailed again, getting closer. D'Amico looked wildly around him but the girl had disappeared. The three men rushed for the door. Hank and I stared at Harris, whose head was tilted crazily into the blood and brain matter that had welled out onto the cushion.

27

The flak that followed took time and money to sort out and involved Viv Garner, my lawyer, Hank's lawyer, Gerard Fonteyn and his legal team and phone calls, texts and emails too numerous to count.

Technically, I could have been considered guilty of various offences: concealing evidence of a crime—the death of the man (a watchman in Philip Harris's employ who'd apparently been bribed by Lance) at the Centennial Park house; restraint of liberty in respect of Harris; possession of an unlicensed firearm (Harris's pistol). But being able to identify who had committed two murders more or less negated the first offence. With Harris dead there was no way to prove I'd taken him against his will and my claim that I was dealing with a medical emergency had evidence to support it after the autopsy. Tests showed that Harris had fired the pistol and sustained my claim that it was his gun.

My statement accused Harris of killing Paul D'Amico, which got that case off the books for the Queensland police. I claimed to have no knowledge of who killed Desiree; I wasn't going to open that can of worms. The upshot was a black mark against Hank for his association with me (his first) and another one for me—one of many.

Investigation revealed that George D'Amico had left Australia within hours of killing Harris and his whereabouts were unknown.

After affirming that I'd been working for him and had kept him informed of my investigation almost up to the fatal events of that night, Fonteyn was understandably chilly. While I could argue that I had confirmed that his daughter was alive I couldn't claim that I'd offered her any protection. His daughter and his son were loose somewhere and both obviously in danger in different ways.

Fonteyn cancelled my line of credit. Megan was annoyed with me for involving Hank in the schemozzle, and Colin Cameron was furious about losing his shot at the big time. The story had made the news services and I even had an angry phone call from Philip Harris who, for all his antipathy towards him, hadn't wanted his brother's brains blown out and for his property to bear the stain of being a murder site.

That's how uncomfortably and humiliatingly matters stood for a week or so before I got a phone call from Fonteyn.

'Mr Hardy, I'm calling to apologise.'

'That's not necessary.'

'It is. I was hasty. You're the only one who made any progress in this matter. You established that Juliana was still alive. When I cooled down I appreciated that.'

'Alive, but . . .'

'Somewhere and I want to recommission you to find her and Foster. Are you willing to try?'

What could I say? The man had played straight with me from the first. It was a tall order, perhaps impossible to carry out, but I felt an obligation and hadn't given the thing up in my head. I'd briefly had control of Foster and had lost him. He was an adult, just, but I should have taken precautions and hadn't. I'd had no control over Juliana but she was a child and failing to find and protect her sat very uneasily with me.

'I'll try,' I said.

'Thank you. I'm grateful to you for keeping Foster more or less out of things. Do you have any idea . . .?'

'He's back in the drug world, Mr Fonteyn.'

'He had a part in Juliana's disappearance, didn't he?'

'I'm afraid so.'

I didn't tell him how big a part and how much things in his family had got off-track; he could wait for those blows if I managed to find either one of his children.

'As to money . . .' Fonteyn said.

'Later, Mr Fonteyn, later.'

I got busy. I put out feelers to a drug counsellor I knew who worked in the eastern suburbs to see if she knew anything about a pusher named Jake. She didn't. I talked to a couple of people I'd seen in the initial part of my first investigation, in case Juliana had been in touch, with no result. I left a photograph of Foxy at the Double Bay café and one of Juliana at the Waverley hotel with the promise of a reward for information. I got no response.

Then Bruce McBain, the Coolangatta boat dealer, rang me. I thought I was going to be in for more abuse but not so.

'I still think you're a bastard, Hardy, but you've done me a favour and I'm going to repay it.'

'I'm not aware of doing you any favours. I thought I told you to take a long holiday.'

'You did. I left briefly, but now I'm back because the air has cleared.'

'How's that?'

'I followed the news. D'Amico has left the country with a murder charge hanging over him, right?'

'Right.'

'So I'm safe from him. The bonus is that Cantini's gone as well. His connections with D'Amico came to light and his enemies started talking. He's resigned and done a flit. I've had trouble with that crooked bastard for years and I'm glad to be rid of him.'

'I can imagine. Well, good luck to you. I could do with some good news myself.'

'I'm not sure how good it is but when he was in Sydney, it must've been just before you . . . before he was killed . . .

Harris phoned and changed his plans and arranged for his boat to be taken to Sydney. When I read what had happened to him I decided to release the boat anyway, to . . . clear the decks, you might say.'

He laughed at his own joke, a happy man.

'Who did you release it to?'

'Bloke named Mathieson. Mick Mathieson. I know him; he's worked on charter boats around here for years. Good sailor. Harris said Mick owed him a favour and that he was posting a cheque to me for the docking charges and some repairs. The cheque took a while to get here and to clear but it did and Mick got to work on the boat. Got it ready and took off.'

'When was this?'

'Day before yesterday. I thought about it before I decided to call you but you never know when doing a favour for someone like you might prove useful in these hard times. We've had some bad weather off the coast to the south that'll slow Mick down and might make him put in somewhere. But the northerlies and westerlies are due about now and they'll send him on his way.'

'How long?'

'Hmm, five hundred nautical miles, near enough. Depends on how she performs and how hard he pushes her. At a guess, another five or six days.'

'I don't suppose you know where he's going to end up, exactly?'

He laughed again, Jolly Bruce McBain. 'He's bound for Botany Bay.'

I asked McBain if he knew why Harris had changed his mind about selling his yacht and he said he didn't.

'Lance loved that boat. Maybe he just couldn't bear to part with it.'

'Or he didn't need the money.'

'You'd know more about that than me.'

I got a description of Mathieson from McBain and asked whether it was possible to sail the *Zaca 3* to Sydney single-handed.

'For Mick Mathieson? Sure.'

He rang off and I sat back and thought about it. Had Harris told Juliana at some point about the boat being brought to Sydney? There was a chance that he had once he'd put her under lock and key. He was the gloating type and he'd said she knew the *whole score*. It was a reasonable bet—especially after he'd betrayed her—that she'd make a try for the boat. I supposed there were marinas and moorings in Botany Bay and I had a few days to work with before the *Zaca* was due.

I arranged a meeting with Gerard Fonteyn at his office and told him about the development.

'You're a yachtsman, Mr Fonteyn,' I said. 'I want to enlist your help to find the boat. I believe she'll try to get it, either to sell it or to . . . go somewhere. I understand there are quite a few moorings in Botany Bay.'

He looked older and greyer than when I'd first met him but his body language was positive and his mind was as alert as ever.

'Yes, certainly, but that's not the only reason you've told me this.'

'True. I feel you have a right to be involved at this point, because what we're actually doing is setting a trap for your daughter. It could be dangerous, depending on the company she's keeping and her state of mind. There could be a need for negotiation. Best if you were personally involved.'

'Supposing this works and Juliana does get to the boat, shouldn't the police be included?'

'Possibly. Again, that'd be up to you.'

'Perhaps the police should be notified at this point.'

'Perhaps.'

'But you don't think so.'

'Too much to go wrong. After all the noise about Harris's killing this is still a live story. If we alert the police now and it leaks to the media, the man controlling the boat might be frightened off and Juliana might change her mind. Or both.'

'Well, I'll do what I can to locate the boat. When is it due to arrive?'

'Hard to say. The best guess is another few days.'

'And I'll think hard about the police when—and if—we reach a crucial point. Thank you, Mr Hardy.'

'Don't thank me yet. It's no more than a possibility and there's no definite plan for the next step, even if it works.'

'Nevertheless, I'm hopeful. Ah . . . what about Foster?'

I shook my head and he nodded solemnly. There was nothing else to say.

28

Sitting and waiting is one of the things I do worst. I was worried about Colin Cameron. I was sure he'd have photos of me in conversation with Harris and, having followed my investigation since Norfolk Island, he had other photos and information that would allow him to cobble together a story he could sell about the Juliana Fonteyn case. I needed to keep him in line and the best way to do that was to hold out renewed hope for his great coup.

'Thanks for keeping quiet about me,' he said when I phoned him.

'Are you being ironic? I thought you might fancy the notoriety.'

'Not just now, thanks. Given my visa, the last thing I need is attention from the authorities.'

'Come on, this government doesn't do nasty things to people with pale skins and freckles who speak with English accents.'

'That's as may be. Anyway, to what do I owe the honour?'

I gave him an outline of the way things stood and told him Gerard Fonteyn would stick to the agreement to let him talk to Juliana if she came through intact.

'What about being in on the denouement?'

'I can't promise that, things might happen very quickly. But I'll keep it in mind.'

'I got a good close-up of the boat when it was moored in Coolangatta. Could that help?'

'It might, yes.'

'I'll send it.'

That seemed enough to keep him sweet. My next call was to Hank, who said he was standing by.

'What about Megan?'

'She understands and she forgives you. She tells me to be careful.'

'We both have to be careful. If Juliana shows up in company I'll probably need you; if she shows up alone you can fade away and I'll shout dinner at Thai Pothong.'

I went back to doing what I do badly, but not for long. Having a drink in the Toxteth hotel I bumped into Joe Chambers. I'd paid for Foxy's stay and the cleaning bill so we were on good terms again.

'I saw that low-life who went off with your Mr Charles Foster,' he said.

'You did? Where? When was this?'

'Yesterday evening. I was walking my dog and I saw him on a seat in Foley Park. He had a couple of plastic bags and a sleeping bag. I think he's dossing there.'

'It's a stone's throw from the cop shop.'

'There's places you could get out of sight. Anyway, just thought I'd mention it.'

I bought him a drink and pressed him for a detailed description of the man. A close observer of humankind in his way, Joe was able to provide it—tall, thin, straggly beard, shoulder-length dark hair, dark cargo shorts, denim jacket.

It was after ten o'clock on a cool but clear night. I went home, got a torch and walked the several blocks back to the park on the corner of Glebe Point and Bridge roads. The restaurants and cafés in the vicinity were doing business, but quietly, and traffic was light. The park had recently undergone renovation, with the war memorial being cleaned up and more benches (with dividers in the middle to deter sleepers) installed and some attention had been paid to the garden beds. As a resident and ratepayer I'd taken a casual look at it after the refit and had a good idea where a person might sleep rough in concealment. The street lights didn't have much effect other than to cast long shadows and the park was quite dark. Using the torch, I followed the path from the memorial to a point where the garden grew densely and head-high between the path and the wall that bordered the park. A loud snore told me I was on the right track.

I moved closer, pushed aside some branches and the torch beam hit a figure huddled in a sleeping bag beside the wall.

Crouching, I moved up beside him and shook his shoulder. He stirred and I shone the torch directly into his face. He jerked awake, blinking furiously and trying to shield his eyes.

'What the fuck . . .'

'Take it easy,' I said. 'I'm not going to hurt you or cause you any trouble. I just want to know where Foxy Fonteyn is.'

'Who?'

'I take back what I said. I will hurt you if you lie to me. You met up with him a while back and you both got high in his apartment in Forest Lodge. Then you both took off. Where is he?'

He was a weedy, under-nourished twenty-year-old or thereabouts and having a big man carrying a heavy torch looming over him wasn't something he could cope with. His breath was rank and his sleeping bag smelled of urine. His beard was crusted with whatever he'd last eaten. I calculated where his right knee was and brought the torch down on it hard. He yelped.

I used the light to turn on my voice recorder and then trained it on him again. 'I'll repeat the question. Where is Foster Fonteyn?'

'Take the fuckin' torch away. Foxy's dead, man. He's gone.'

He told me he and Fonteyn had drifted around eking out the money I'd laid out, spending it mostly on booze and drugs.

'Foxy heard the news about this missing chick who'd turned up and then vanished and he said it was his sister. They said she was from a wealthy family and I said he should get in touch and, you know, score some dough. He said he couldn't do that. He didn't tell me why, or if he did, I forget. We were both pretty fucked up. He was depressed and always going on about how guilty he felt and about something . . . yeah, swimming.'

'Swimming?'

'Said he and his sister were great swimmers. Who the fuck cares? Anyway, we ended up at Maroubra Beach one night, by the rocks there, with some smack and pills. I was feeling crook and didn't want any. Foxy shot up and took the pills. Then he said he was going to swim to New Zealand. Man, he was wrecked. Off his face.'

'Go on.'

'He crawled down to the water, clothes, boots and all, and went in and started swimming and he was right, he could fuckin' swim. But, shit, not with that load on. He got a fair way out but I've got good eyes. I saw him go under twice and come up but the last time he didn't come up.'

'I haven't heard of a body being washed ashore.'

'Are they always?'

I had to admit I didn't know. They never found Harold Holt or Commander Crabb. But I knew Maroubra Beach and its rips and currents. Foxy could well be on his way to New Zealand, but he'd never see it.

'You didn't try to stop him?'

He looked at me with genuine puzzlement. 'Why would I do that? He's better off.'

I could see his point. 'What's your name?'

'Travis Wilson.'

'ID.'

He fished out a long-expired student card with a photograph that still resembled him, but only just. I gave him twenty dollars and left him there. I believed him and so would anyone listening to the recording; he didn't have the imagination to invent such a story and some of the details rang true.

I walked home and a light rain that would make it uncomfortable for him began to fall. Now I had information for Gerard Fonteyn but the question was when to give it to him—before or after the idea I was working on played out? The man with the Midas touch seemed to be paying for his good fortune bit by bit.

29

Gerard Fonteyn rang me four days later.

'The *Zaca* is due to arrive in two days,' he said.

'How do you know that?'

'I have contacts. She has a mooring booked at the South Botany Sailing Club down near Sandringham Bay. Do you know where that is?'

'Not really. Somewhere around Ramsgate?'

'That's right. The skipper will contact the yacht-club secretary twelve hours before he's due in. That's the protocol. When he does, the secretary will contact me. What's our plan?'

As I expected, he intended to be on the spot. And he'd earned the right.

'We're hoping Harris told her where the boat was coming to. Or he might have mentioned it earlier. Maybe it's a favourite mooring of his. She'll only have a rough idea of when but if I'm right that she'll target the boat, she'd be likely to keep her eye on the South Botany Club. She knows about yachts, maybe she could get someone to tell her when the *Zaca*'s called in.'

Fonteyn could see the thinness of this as much as I could and he had to challenge it. 'You're assuming that she's . . . functional.'

'She looked okay in the brief glimpse I got of her and she was alert enough to take advantage of a pretty brief distraction. She's been through a lot. We just have to hope that it's toughened her up. It's all we've got.'

'So, do we post people there now to look out for her?'

'I don't think so. There's any number of places she could watch from without being obvious. I'll take a good look myself first. Our best bet is to take her when she breaks cover and goes for the boat.'

As soon as I spoke I realised what a poor choice of words I'd made. I was treating his child as prey. I muttered an apology but Fonteyn was a master of his emotions. His voice was steady when he replied.

'Do you expect any trouble from Mathieson?'

'It's hard to say. If he's heard that Harris's dead he'll probably just dock the boat, deposit the documents and get out. If he hasn't, he'll most likely wait around for a while for Harris to show up. If he starts asking questions . . .'

'All right,' Fonteyn said. 'We have things to deal with and we will. I still have the option to call in the police.'

I bit the bullet. 'I have some information that may help you decide that. We'd better have a meeting.'

Fonteyn was at home helping to take care of his wife, who, he told me, was seriously ill. It seemed as though his debt to fortune was getting heavier by the minute. I drove to Vaucluse. When I announced my arrival the big gate opened and I parked in front of the house sprawled at the top of the bluff. Nothing ostentatious, just big, well-maintained in every way and singing of good taste and money.

Fonteyn met me at the door and escorted me through to his study—book-lined somewhat untidily and with a view out over the water that would have stopped me thinking. When I asked after his wife he just shook his head. We sat in comfortable chairs. I refused coffee and produced my voice recorder.

'I'm sorry, bad news,' I said. 'Prepare yourself.'

He nodded. 'Foster?'

'Yes, I'm sorry.'

I switched on the recorder and put it on the edge of the desk close to where he sat. Because the device is so small he automatically leaned a little towards it although the volume was up enough to be easily heard. As the voice stumbled on he gradually sank back in the chair. When it finished I turned the recorder off and I said I was sorry again.

He'd heard the last few exchanges with his eyes closed. Now he opened them and lifted his head to gaze out the window but I doubt he was taking in anything of that magnificent view.

He pointed to the recorder. 'You believe him?'

'Yes, he's very damaged but not capable of inventing something like that. It rings true.'

'Poor boy. I let him down by . . . pushing him. His mother warned me but I was busy and took no notice. From what you've told me, I didn't do well by Juliana either.'

I'd given him an edited version of what his son had told me about Juliana's reaction to life in the Vaucluse house.

'In a different way,' I said. 'But it's not too late to make amends there.'

'Which brings us to the South Botany Sailing Club and my call on whether to involve the police.'

'That's right. I'm not saying the police aren't competent. Some are, but not all and we'd have no control over the people they'd use.'

'And they carry guns.'

'Well, it'd be all square on that count; I'd have one, too. The trouble is the police know about Harris from earlier episodes and they'd link the boat and anyone associated with it with drugs. Given their own record in that area, drugs make them anxious. They're brainwashed about them and tend to be hard-line; it starts at the Academy.'

'I thought that was changing.'

'Slowly.'

'All right. Anything else against using the police?'

I shrugged. 'It's doubtful they'd let you play an active role.'

'So your advice would be to handle it privately.'

'Yes.'

Fonteyn hadn't got to where he was by being indecisive. He said, 'I'll get that twelve-hour alert and let you know. Then I'll leave those details to you, but I want to be there at the earliest appropriate moment.'

That was said with something of his customary force but there was an understandable air of reduction about him. I felt that the future of his life hung on the success of this gambit. My stake was less but still big enough.

I hit the Princes Highway and took it south through Rockdale until the turn-off towards Botany Bay. There were a couple of sailing and yachting clubs along the coast, always set in parklands with large parking areas. A few kilometres inland from here there was bland suburbia but on the beach there was money and signs of it being spent—on big houses in bad taste with a penchant for pillars.

South Botany was on a smaller scale than some of the other clubs and had a more practical air. The clubhouse was modest and the car park could have done with a bit of work. There was the usual flagpole with the Australian flag but as I parked my eye was caught by a huge anchor painted white and set on a cement plinth. The plaque revealed it to be a relic from a naval vessel I should have heard of, but hadn't.

I wandered around in the mild, breezy air without anyone taking any notice of me. Adjacent to the clubhouse there were a couple of shops, one dealing in sailing clothing and the other in boat hardware. There was a smallish jetty out into the water and off to one side were two slipways with yachts drawn up and being worked on. The couple of moorings beside the jetty were fully occupied but a scattering of other boats was moored twenty or so metres out into the little protective inlet. Dinghies bobbed astern of them or were drawn up and stowed on the decks. Altogether a perfect place for a discreet aquatic arrival. My survey confirmed the impression I'd had from the web that, from not-far-distant higher points, it'd be possible to watch with a pair of binoculars without being seen.

I went into the hardware place, remembering it was called a ship's chandler, and inspected some of the gear, most of which was as foreign to me as aeronautical equipment.

'Can I help you?'

A young woman in jeans and a T-shirt bobbed up from behind the counter.

'Not at the moment,' I said. 'Maybe in the future. I understand there are moorings for hire here.'

'A few.' She pointed out the window at the boats I'd seen. 'They go pretty fast.'

'It looks fairly full.'

'There's a few not taken, but they'd mostly be booked.'

I thanked her and went back to the car. Although it was an ideal place for the *Zaca* to put in, it wasn't right for a couple of men the size of Hank and an individual of Fonteyn's appearance to hang about as a reception committee. We'd have to take advantage of the hiding places ourselves and dress the part.

30

I got a call from Fonteyn at 6.00 pm.

His voice was tight with tension. 'The *Zaca*'s twelve hours out.'

'Right,' I said. 'Cancel everything you have on for the day and get some rest.'

'As if I could.'

'Try and be down there an hour earlier but not before that. I'll meet you. Dress casually.'

'D'you think I'd wear a suit?'

'Mr Fonteyn, every one of us, Juliana included, is going to be on edge. We have to be cool and cooperative if this is going to work.'

It's not every day you get to dictate terms to a multi-millionaire but he grunted some kind of assent and hung up. I'd drawn out a thousand dollars of his money as an inducement to Mick Mathieson if that was needed. Then

234

I phoned Hank and went over the plan, such as it was, with him. I visited the gym, had a focaccia and a glass of wine at the Bar Napoli and went for a long walk to tire myself before going to bed but I slept badly, waking several times before the alarm went off.

Hank collected me in his Kombi van. This would allow us to squat in the back in reasonable comfort and without attracting attention.

Dawn was a good hour away. We took a position in the public car park that left us 150 metres, give or take, away from the South Botany clubhouse and slipway but with a clear view out into the mooring areas where boats were bobbing in water stirred up by currents and a slight breeze. The breeze had a cold edge. No view yet to speak of but a light on the clubhouse and distant street lamps gave an indication of what the scene would be when the sun came up. The forecast had promised a clear day with temperatures in the low twenties. We sat in the van drinking coffee from a thermos I'd brought and didn't say anything.

The sky lightened at about 5.30 and there was no sign of Fonteyn. Hank looked questioningly at me and I shrugged. With the light gathering strength, a few yachties who'd evidently spent the night on their boats emerged and started doing the things yachties do.

A few minutes later a couple of gardeners showed up in a council vehicle. They parked well away from us and began offloading tools. Then two cars pulled into the clubhouse car park and I saw the woman I'd spoken to go to her shop. Two men got out of the other car. One went into the clubhouse and switched on more lights, the other unlocked the gate that secured the slipway and rolled it back. He stalked around, talking on his mobile phone. With so much activity going on I risked stepping down from the Kombi and looking around. It was 5.40. A figure emerged from the parkland, middle-sized, in dark clothes and wearing a cap. It paused to allow a couple of early joggers to pass and then approached me. It was Fonteyn.

'Timing right?' he said. 'Discreet enough?'

I nodded. At the Kombi I introduced him to Hank. Fonteyn took binoculars from his jacket pocket and slung them around his neck. Then he produced a flask and passed it around. We each had a slug of the strong, smooth spirit.

'Now what?' Fonteyn said.

I said, 'There's probably enough activity about for us to get closer and take a good look. One at a time and then wander off.'

Hank pointed to where a couple of pelicans had settled on the end of the small jetty. 'Are you a birdwatcher, Mr Fonteyn?' Hank said.

'I can be today.'

And that's how we played it for over an hour.

*

Day broke and the area around the clubhouse and on the slipway and in the water got busy. Good for not attracting attention to us but we became anxious as the time dragged on.

'I don't suppose anything is ever precise with yacht arrivals,' I said.

Fonteyn seemed the calmest of us and I wondered whether it was due to self-control or scepticism about our plan. With a man like him it was hard to tell.

'Absolutely not,' Fonteyn said. 'Too many variables—wind, use of engine, condition of the . . .'

Hank had been on watch. He came hurrying back and handed his Canon binoculars to me. 'You know what she looks like, Cliff,' he said. 'There's something out there.'

Fonteyn swung his binoculars forward. 'I've seen the photographs. I'll know.'

'How long between when she comes into view and when she reaches the mooring?' I said.

Fonteyn was on the move. 'Same question, same answer as before,' he said over his shoulder. 'Too many variables.' He moved quickly down into the best watching position and Hank and I fanned out behind him. We watched him scan the water, which had taken on a green tinge under the sun and was lapping at the shore and slipway in small waves. Fonteyn strolled back to us. 'Have you got money for this man?'

'I've got a thousand bucks of your money.' I produced the bundle of notes and he took it.

237

'I'll match it. I'll double it if I have to.'

'We'll see,' I said. I trained my glasses on the speck far out that was gradually increasing in size and definition.

'Yes,' Fonteyn said. 'I'll just have a word with someone in the club.'

He strode to the steps and went up to the clubhouse, an assured figure, taking off his cap and patting down his hair.

'He'll smooth things,' Hank said. 'That guy knows what he's doing.'

'He fucked up his whole family,' I said, 'and I don't think he'd agree with you, but he's trying, he's certainly trying.'

We watched the *Zaca* draw closer; she appeared to zig and zag a few times and I suppose that was what was meant by tacking, but she came on steadily and in a stately fashion.

'Nice boat,' Hank said.

'Nice price,' I grunted. 'I wonder how Harris managed to afford it.'

'Drug money, I guess. Just as well you didn't bring the cops in on this. They'd likely confiscate it as something bought with the proceeds of crime.'

Eventually the yacht glided to a halt about 200 metres from the jetty and I saw a man go quickly into the cabin, then come out again and take a position on watch over the side.

'Anchor was on an electric switch,' Hank said. 'Classy.'

I looked at him. 'You didn't tell me you knew about yachts.'

Hank grinned. 'I know bugger-all but I looked a few things up.'

The man, in jeans and a sweater and wearing a beanie, did things with ropes and then paid another quick visit to the cabin. A dinghy held at the stern of the yacht slid down into the water.

'Five gets you ten it's got an outboard,' Hank said.

He was right. The sailor dropped down into the trailing dinghy; the motor started easily and the dinghy came briskly towards the jetty, its occupant skilfully avoiding the moored boats. He tied up and climbed onto the deck with some rolled-up papers in his hand.

'What now?' Hank said. 'Intercept him?'

I considered, then shook my head. 'Let Fonteyn handle it.'

31

After what seemed like a long wait but was probably only a quarter of an hour, Fonteyn and the man who had to be Mick Mathieson emerged from the clubhouse and shook hands. Mathieson headed for the road beyond the park, working at his mobile phone as he went. Hank and I retreated to the Kombi and Fonteyn joined us there.

'A reasonable enough chap,' he said. 'Relieved not to have to deal with Harris—no love lost there. But he was worried about what might lie in store until I . . . reassured him.'

'And now?' I said.

Fonteyn took a deep breath and passed the flask around again. 'They tell me inside that a young woman has been making enquiries about the yacht for a week or more. She comes jogging through the park at around eight o'clock.'

'Description?' I asked.

'Tall, tanned with cropped hair and,' he touched his left nostril and lower lip, 'with rings, but fit, very fit.'

We had almost an hour to wait and again it passed very slowly. A few minutes before eight Hank said quietly, 'How do we handle it if she shows?'

'She'll get close enough to identify the yacht,' I said. 'She'll know the dinghy is at the jetty and that's where she'll go. Fonteyn and I'll brace her there and not give her time to untie the dinghy. She has two avenues of escape if that's what she wants to do—to swim or to dodge us and run. If she swims I don't know what the hell we do; if she gets past us you can restrain her, Hank. She's underage, her father can give you the authority.'

Fonteyn hated it but he nodded.

She came at 8.15, a tall, lithe figure in a tracksuit and sneakers, moving like Cathy Freeman. Her short hair was dyed auburn. She stopped, performed a few stretches and looked out over the water. Fonteyn and I were twenty-five metres away off to the right and as she walked down the cement path towards the jetty we fell in behind her a couple of metres apart and apparently on our own business. She didn't look behind her and as soon as she stepped onto the jetty we ran and were only a couple of metres from her when she spun around.

'Juliana!' Fonteyn shouted and then repeated the name in a harsh whisper.

She turned to look out at the yacht and then turned back, balanced at her full imposing height.

'Hello, Dad,' she said. 'Nice to see you, I suppose.'

'I . . . I . . .' Fonteyn stuttered.

We were now just beyond arm's length from her and I could tell that Fonteyn wanted to reach out to her but something told him not to. Juliana looked at me.

'Who's this?'

'My name's Hardy, Ms Fonteyn. I'm a private detective your father hired to look for you.'

'Oh, yeah. I've got you now. You were there when Lance got shot.'

'That's right. I've tracked you from Norfolk Island to Coolangatta to here.'

'Good for you. What now?'

Fonteyn recovered himself as he always would and said, 'That's up to you, darling. I'm just relieved to know you're alive. I don't want you to do anything you don't want to do.'

She looked down to where the dinghy was bumping gently against the pylons of the jetty. 'That's a first.'

'I know. I'm sorry.'

'That's a first, too.'

'Your brother's dead.'

'I know. I'm sorry, sort of.'

'You've seen Travis Wilson,' I said.

'Yeah, and Jake, and all that bunch.'

Fonteyn looked enquiringly at me.

'Addicts and pushers,' I said.

'That's right,' Juliana said. 'But I cut loose from all of them and I've kicked all the shit.'

'What're you doing now?' Fonteyn said quietly.

She stepped back and for an instant I thought she was going to either run or attack us but she mimed a perfect top-spin backhand.

'I'm working as a part-time tennis and swimming coach.'

'You're too young. You have no qualifications.'

She smiled. 'False ID, Dad. It's the real world.'

I had to admire Fonteyn. He didn't try to lay any guilt on her about the suffering he'd been through or the expense or the loss of his son, which could in a way be construed as collateral damage.

'Tell me what you want, Juliana,' he said.

She drew herself up. She'd grown in the time she'd been on the loose and at about 183 centimetres she was able to stare her father straight in the face.

'I'll tell you what I want, *Daddy*. What I'm here to do. I want to take that yacht out into Botany Bay and scuttle the fucker.'

With an obvious effort, Fonteyn prevented himself from flinching at her language.

'Will you come back?'

'You'll let me do it?'

'If that's what you want.'

She looked at me and over my shoulder at Hank, who wasn't far away.

'What about them?'

'They work for me.'

She looked down the jetty. 'The dinghy's there.'

After a tense moment she said, 'Okay . . . and then I'll think about what to do next.'

Fonteyn took a key attached to a heavy wooden tag and handed it to her. She avoided his hand but touched his arm quickly and sprang away to go down the short ladder. We all stood stock still as we heard the outboard fire and saw the dinghy pull away in a swish of oily water.

Hank drifted away to leave Fonteyn and me to watch as the dinghy reached the yacht. Juliana climbed aboard, tied up to the stern and within a few minutes had raised the anchor and had the *Zaca* heading for the open water.

'Unwise, d'you think?' Fonteyn said.

'Can't say. I can't think of a precedent to guide me.'

His chuckle was more to break the tension than a sign of amusement. 'She looks well, doesn't she? Older.'

'Yes, and perhaps wiser. How long does it take to scuttle a boat?'

He shrugged.

'About?' I said.

'Depends. Half an hour, give or take.'

'Won't she be spotted?'

His face was a mask of concern. 'To tell you the truth I don't really know her anymore. But from the way she's coped with everything so far I think she'll take care not to be seen.'

'You know what she's doing, don't you?' I said.

He nodded. 'The boat's where she encountered someone who showed her how dark things can be. She wants to wipe the slate clean. My worry is that she's committing a serious crime.'

'Only technically,' I said. 'Harris probably bought the yacht with money earned by selling drugs. It's forfeit on that account anyway.'

'That's a point. Still, I'm sure what she's doing breaks some maritime law. I just hope she's careful.'

I could imagine insurance and dumping-at-sea problems if it all came out. Fonteyn's money would help solve them but my concern was different.

'My worry is whether she'll come back or take off. It's a big stretch of water and she could go ashore anywhere.'

The yacht was out of sight now and Fonteyn lowered the glasses.

'I know,' he said. 'But I felt I had to give her that chance, although it went against all my . . . civil instincts to do it. I'm going to be a different man after this experience, however it turns out.'

I believed him but I thought he'd find changing the habits of twenty years harder than he realised. If Juliana came back he'd face a challenge greater than any he'd had in the academic or commercial world.

The sky clouded over and the day became cooler but neither of us, off the jetty now and sitting on a bench wrapped in our own thoughts, really felt the difference. We were transfixed by the slowly darkening water. Eventually Fonteyn, who had better vision than me, raised the glasses.

'What?' I said.

He didn't answer; he just kept the glasses trained steadily over the water until even I could see the dinghy making its way back towards the moorings.

'I can see her clearly now,' Fonteyn said, 'and she's smiling.'

He lowered the glasses and shook my hand. He was smiling and so was I.